# The Dream Weaver

## By Imogen Aldridge

WYNWORD
PRESS

*The Dream Weaver*

## WYNWORD PRESS

PO Box 557
Bonners Ferry, ID 83805
www.wynwordpress.com

Distributed by Wynword Press

Cover Art: David Meister

Printed in the U.S.A.

ISBN 978-1-940638-02-7

❦ In loving memory of Derrick John Meister ❧

How do I best honor your life, Der? For me, it might be trying to herd the carpenter ants outside so we don't have to kill them.

I'm so glad I knew you. Happy Birthday, Der. I hope you like the story.

# Prologue:

# ✁ The Loom ✂

There aren't too many folks that use a back-strap loom these days, at least, I never met anyone besides myself. So I guess I'd better tell you a little about it.

A back-strap loom is an ancient type of loom still used by weavers in South America. The weaver, herself, is part of the loom, and uses her body to maintain tension on the warps. The loom is made from several sticks and some ropes or straps. The sticks are used to anchor and organize the warps, which are the vertical threads of the weaving. The weft, or horizontal thread, is passed over and under alternate warps to form a web.

Heddles are used to form the sheds. The simplest sheds consist of every other warp. These are alternately lifted up and dropped down so the weft can pass over or under each of them. This way, the weaver doesn't have to pass the weft over and under individual warps. She opens a shed and passes the weft between the lower and upper warps. Then she closes the shed, beats that weft against the already-woven part of the web, opens the alternate shed and passes the weft through again.

Harness looms can have several sheds. A back-strap loom, also, can have several, but usually has only two. One is created with a stick that floats in the weaving, being pushed up the length of the warps as the web gets longer. This is called the stick heddle. The other is called the string heddle. It consists of loops of string that are passed over certain warps, enabling the weaver to pull them up by pulling on the strings. These strings are then passed over another stick so they can all be raised together by pulling on the stick.

*The Dream Weaver*

When the weaver weaves, she holds the warps taut by tying the top loom stick to a stout post or tree. The bottom stick is secured to the weaver by passing a strap around her back, which is tied to each end of the bottom stick. She adjusts the tension on the warps by leaning closer or further away from the stationary post to make it easier to open the sheds and balance the warp and weft.

# Chapter 1

## ✶ Danny and Momma ✶

My hands are old now, and gnarled as crooked twigs. On frosty Idaho mornings, I can hardly bend them without feeling the ache in my knuckles. Or even if I can, a couple of fingers might get stuck, curled up and locked like handcuffs snapping shut, and I have to soak them in hot water and rub the joints to get them to open up again.

It's getting harder to weave. My wrists ache when I throw the shuttle between the sheds, and my arm's too weak to pull the string heddle up. I've been working on this web for seven years now. The going's slow and the work intricate, the most intricate I've ever done. Except for this, I pretty much stopped weaving ten years ago, when Virgil died. But I'm determined to finish it, my last and greatest work.

I try to weave a couple of hours every day, though some days it's hard to get my old bones down to the floor. So I skip it and sit in my rocking chair, watching through my double glass doors as the sunrise paints the southern mountains with a golden wash. I make a cup of tea and tell over my memories like fingering beads on a string. It's a long string. I'm 84 years old.

"Why do you still weave on that crazy old loom, Auntie Sairy?" Joleen asks me. "Get yourself a real loom, one with a bench. It'd be easier on your back than that old thing. Plus, it's faster."

Faster. I guess it would be! I weave on a back-strap loom. I learned how as a young girl, taught myself out of a book I checked out of the library. I wanted to weave, and we had no money for fancy equipment. So I found a few sticks in the woods and learned to make a loom out of 'em and weave the old way. When I can get down to my cushion on the floor, and when my hands don't ache too much, I love to weave. I lean forward just a mite to loosen the warp, and then move the heddle stick toward me. I thread the shuttle through the shed, push the heddle stick away, lean back hard and tamp the weft firmly in place with the beater. Then I lean forward again, pull up on the string heddle, pass the shuttle back through and tamp again. The subtle swaying backward and forward, the passing of the weft first this way and then that, comfort me with their slow rhythm. After all these years, my muscles know of their own accord just how much tension to put on the back strap and just how taut to make the weft, though I struggled with that when I first started weaving.

I've never used a harness loom myself, but I've seen folks weave on 'em. I don't know how you'd weave a right dream on one of those. All that clicking and clacking. All those pedals. Weave fabric, sure. But not a dream. Dreams have to unfold over time. It's the minute changes in tension and the tiny threads of color, judiciously added in just the right spots, that make a good dream.

All those dreams I wove across the years, I didn't recognize the thread of evil running through them. No matter how golden a dream is, there's a dark thread locked inexorably between the sheds that cannot be excised without unraveling the whole web.

The only pure dreams, I've come to realize, are the ones that never come true.

*** 

The first thing I ever wove was a strap to hold the loom around my back. Before I made the strap, I had to use a piece of old rope I found lying around the house and stuff a pillow down behind it to keep it from cutting into my back. I wove the strap out of white cotton string and scraps I begged off Momma that were left over from her knitting.

Momma was a knitting fool. We didn't have a radio, so she would sit down in her rocking chair after dinner every night and make those knitting needles fly. One year, she knit 14 sweaters between August and Christmas to give to our relatives and friends. She tried to teach me once, but I'm left-handed and couldn't quite get the hang of it from watching her. Being right handed or left doesn't matter for weaving, so it seemed to me it'd be easier to learn. Not that I picked it up right away, mind you!

I still use that strap I wove for my loom today, and it's a crazy jumble of bare white warps alternating with loose blue and yellow weft, and loops at the edges every so often where I didn't pull the weft across evenly. It's hard to weave a straight piece on a back-strap loom, and I wove many before I learned to do it just right.

After I finished the strap and Momma realized I was serious about weaving, she let me buy my own yarn. We used to go to the dime store, and I'd buy the cheapest yarn I could find: Red Heart worsted yarn. I'd work my tail off, doing laundry, helping with the canning, picking bugs off the string beans, and save up my pennies to buy yarn.

During the day, nobody had time to knit or weave. Momma'd root me out of bed early to split kindling for the cook stove. Summer and winter she'd be up at 4:30. "Sairy! Sairy! Time to get up. We need kindling if we're going to have breakfast!"

So I'd stumble out to the back porch and split up sticks to start the fire. My brother stayed in bed while me and Momma made breakfast. She'd send me out to the pump for water while she slammed around the cast-iron skillet and laid out slices of bread to toast on the stovetop. Then I'd go to the chicken coop to throw out grain and see if there were any eggs yet. In the winter, their water would freeze hard during the night, and I'd chip it out of the pan and run in fresh, three times a day during cold spells, so the chickens'd have something to drink.

I still keep chickens. There's something comforting about the sounds they make, even their peevish "wraaaaaaack, wraaaaaaack" when you bump them off the nest to steal their eggs. Those chickens are so stupid they've never lost their fear of me even though I feed 'em day in and day out until they keel over dead from old age. Oh, they waddle up as soon as I open the gate, eager for grain or table scraps, but just try to reach down and touch one! They yowl like a cat under a steamroller and scatter in a hundred different directions.

Momma didn't run an old-age farm for chickens like I do. She wasn't sentimental. When they quit laying, we'd stew them up and eat them. In our house, everyone paid their way. Except my brother. I don't know why he got to laze around in bed while I fed the chickens and fetched water. He always was Momma's favorite.

She wanted a boy so bad, she must've been disappointed when she got me, instead. I guess when he came along two years later, it was Hallelujah time. He could do no wrong. After breakfast was done, when Momma was ready to sit down at the table with a cup of mint tea, she'd send me up to roust him out of bed. He didn't wake up easy, either.

"Get. Up." I'd say. "Time for breakfast, lazy."

"Go 'way," he'd say, pulling the blankets over his head. Or he'd pretend to be asleep and say nothing at all.

Sometimes, I'd get so sick of him snuggling back down in his blanket after I'd been up in the morning cold for an hour already that I'd roll him out onto the floor and grab his blankets away.

"There." I'd say. "Let's see you sleep now. I'm putting your blankets out the window."

He'd wake up and holler, then. "Mooommaaaaaa! Sairy knocked me out of bed!"

"I did not! Danny wouldn't get up!"

We'd both go tumbling down the stairs, clamoring "Did too!" and "Did not!" until Momma fixed me with a baleful glare and said "Be nice to your brother, Sairy. You're the oldest; stop acting like a baby."

Then she'd smooth down his blond cowlick and kiss his forehead. "Don't fret, honey," she'd say. "Sit down at the table and let Momma get you some breakfast."

But he'd fret anyway, say the eggs were runny or the toast was cold. Runny. Huh. She'd cook those eggs so hard they'd bounce off the floor. Never mind that *I* didn't like hard eggs. If I'd been the one complaining, Momma would've said, "We're not running a restaurant here, Sairy." But for Danny, she just shoveled 'em back into the skillet and put down some new bread. She and I ate the cold toast while Danny picked at the fresh.

"He's delicate, Sairy," Momma would say. "Your brother isn't sturdy like you."

I guess she knew better than me…he was fragile, just like she said. He's been dead a good, long time now, got taken early in a road accident. I miss him. Back then, though, I wished he *would* die. Then, maybe Momma would wake up and realize she loved me, too.

After breakfast, I'd take Danny upstairs and stuff him into his school clothes. Or, if it was summer, he'd clean his room, or read, or Momma would make me ride him downtown on my handlebars for Scouts or 4-H or baseball. I don't know why she bothered. He was horrible at baseball, and he hated Scouts and 4-H. He missed half the games and most of the camping trips anyway, what with earaches and colds and stomach flu, all of which plagued him constantly.

"Do I hafta go?" he'd whine, and dawdle around getting his glove or his cap.

Momma, though usually so indulgent, would insist. "Yes. It's good for you to get outdoors. You need some healthy fresh air and sunshine."

"He could get some fresh air and sunshine splitting wood," I'd mumble, but I never said it loud enough for Momma to hear.

Once Danny was dressed, I'd wash up the breakfast dishes. In the summer, washing up was a worse chore because it was uncomfortable standing by the hot stove. I'd throw a couple more sticks on the fire and walk outside to wait until the water got good and hot.

The sun comes up early in the summer. By the time we finished breakfast it would be full daylight and threatening to get hot. I'd try to catch sight of the woodpecker I heard rapping on a dead tree outside the back door, or walk through the woods to see what'd happened there since yesterday. I hated doing housework. I still hate it. I do as little as possible. I try to keep the floor clean near the post I tie my loom to. Other than that, I just let the dust bunnies multiply.

On the days I didn't have to take Danny somewhere, I'd try to disappear so Momma wouldn't find something else for me to do, making bread or scrubbing the floor or washing eggs. Except for Danny, Momma didn't approve of people sitting around gathering wool. She thought they ought to keep busy doing something useful. When there was nothing left for me to do in the house, she'd send me out to the garden with a hoe. I didn't mind that job. I'd pick idly at the weeds and daydream, stopping frequently to estimate how much snow was left on the mountains or slap at a hornet. If Danny'd annoyed me particularly, I'd grumble about it, punctuating each word with a vicious hack at the ground.

"You – spoiled – old – baby," I'd mutter. "I'd – like – to – fix – your – eggs – for – you."

The worst job Momma gave me was mucking out the chicken coop. Chickens're dirty animals, don't have enough sense not to foul their own nests. I'd have to scrape crusted droppings off their perches with a putty knife and dig out the half-composted, stinking straw on the floor. After cleaning the chicken coop, I always changed my dress, couldn't stand the feeling their mess might still be clinging to my clothes.

During the rest of the year, Danny and I would go to school after breakfast. Momma always worried about Danny catching cold. She swathed him in layers of wool from head to toe. I'd put on the mittens she knit me and the hat with earflaps, and, if it was winter, my long underwear, which hung down in baggy folds below my dress, and we'd hike down to the bus stop together. I had to sit with him on the bus, which I hated, because Momma didn't want him getting ragged on by the other kids.

I'd deliver Danny to his class and then go off to mine. I hated school. It bored me, and I wasn't any good at it. Danny was a good student, always brought his report card home proudly, eager to show off his good grades. One time, I stole it out of his coat pocket while we were on the bus and threw it out the window. I figured if he didn't bring his home, she wouldn't get mad at me for not having mine.    I didn't want to show her my Cs and Ds, especially not beside Danny's As. Of course, he told her it was report card day, and when neither one of us could produce a report card, she went to the neighbor's house to call the school office and found out what our grades were. I got in trouble for losing the card, and also for being a bad example for Danny.

When it was recess time at school, I'd slink around the playground trying to stay out of the other kids' way. The younger kids had recess on a different schedule, so at least I didn't have Danny hanging around my neck making me look like a fool. But I didn't have any friends, either.

Most of the other kids lived in town. They didn't wear hand-knit sweaters or long johns hanging out the bottom of their dresses. The girls had store-bought clothes and shiny, patent leather shoes and tights in pretty colors. The boys wore corduroys or stiff, new jeans and flannel shirts. I was the only one with homemade dresses made out of cut-down old lady clothes and worn-out shoes from the second-hand store. I don't guess it was my clothes that made me a pariah, though. I wasn't the only poor kid in school. I just had a hard time warming up to people; I was nervous of 'em. I've always been shy that way.

So I'd stand on the sidelines while the other kids played kick-ball or four square or hopscotch, hoping they'd see me there and invite me to join in.

"Hey, Sairy, you come play on my team," I imagined them saying. "You can play shortstop." But they never did.

After the first few years, I knew they wouldn't notice me and I didn't bother to watch any more. Instead, I roamed around the fence that held in the schoolyard from spilling out into the street. I looked at the ground, mostly, hopeful to find a piece of jewelry someone had dropped, or maybe a toy, and had pretend conversations with my best friend.

"Never mind about that old hopscotch. We don't need all those other girls. Let's play house," my best friend would say.

"No, let's play neighbors. You be Mrs. Colitch and I'll be Mrs. Perdy."

Mrs. Colitch was a formidable lady who went to our church. She wore white gloves and a hat with a veil on it and stared hard down her nose at any children who happened to squirm during the service, like Danny and me.

My best friend would stare down her nose like Mrs. Colitch. "Good morning, Mrs. Perdy. My, what a lovely day it is."

"Yes, indeed, it certainly is, Mrs. Colitch. Shall we have some coffee?"

"Coffee would be lovely. Goodness sakes, who are all those rowdy children over there? Don't their parents teach them any manners?"

"Tsk tsk," I would say, shaking my head. "I don't know what's gotten into young people these days.

"I know your children are beautifully behaved, Mrs. Perdy."

"Yes, they are. I have a problem with Danny every now and again, of course, being a boy and all, but my Sairy is just a delight. And talented. My, oh my. There isn't anything my Sairy can't do."

Then, my best friend would pat her face delicately with a handkerchief and say, "Well, I don't like to mention it to you, Mrs. Perdy. But your Danny was just the teeniest bit rude to me the last week. I had stepped in a little bit of mud on my way into the church, and I got a smear of it on the floor. Well, little Danny was standing in the foyer, fiddling with the guest book, which I must say, Mrs. Perdy, I cannot approve of children playing with the church's guest book. But anyway, I told Danny that if he didn't have anything better to do than play with the guest book, he should get a towel from the kitchen and wipe up the mud so nobody else would step in it. So Danny said, looking right in my face, which I do think is a little disrespectful, if you don't mind my saying so, and said he certainly did have something better to do, ma'am, and slunk off into the sanctuary without ever wiping up the mud. And even though he said 'ma'am', I thought he was quite sassy. And do you know, not two minutes later, Mr. Balridge and his wife came into the foyer and stepped right in that mud. They tracked it halfway to the fellowship hall before Mrs.

Balridge realized what was happening. I thought to myself: Mrs. Perdy would never approve of this type of behavior; I know she wouldn't. Her Sairy is as good as gold."

"I couldn't agree with you more, Mrs. Colitch," I would sigh and shake my head. "It's all I can do to raise that boy right."

Of course, I didn't have a real best friend. The one I had was just in my head. I had to be careful not to talk to her out loud, or the other kids would think I was crazy.

***

I took up weaving as a way to look busy when I was really just daydreaming. The second thing I wove, after the strap, was a scarf for Momma. I did extra chores and saved up my nickels for weeks to buy two skeins of Red Heart, one dark green and one indigo blue. I strung the loom with white cotton string, and started in to make a striped muffler. As I wove, I envisioned Momma's face beaming with pride and heard her voice saying, "You turned out to be the special one after all, Sairy."

One day, after a whole, rainy afternoon at the loom, I looked down at my web to see a tiny, glowing thread of sky blue entwined subtly with the deep hues of blue and green. I wasn't sure how that happened. Maybe Red Heart mixed up the machinery that twisted the strands together, got the wrong color into the skein. I thought maybe I should pull it out, but I'd been so caught up in my fantasy I was an inch past it by the time I saw. I didn't want to go all the way back. I looked closely at the weft yarn I'd wound up on the stick I was using for a shuttle, though, to make sure there weren't any more odd colors there.

The scarf took a long time to finish. It was misshapen, with warps close together and then far apart, and big loops at the selvedge where I'd gotten the tension messed up. It started out fat, then got skinny, then fattened out again, back and forth, back and forth like a stream of clotted milk pouring from a pitcher. It was kind of short, too. Still, I'd been planning to give it to Momma for Christmas and I'd spent all my money on it. I didn't have anything else to give her, so I figured I'd go ahead and wrap it up.

First, though, I carried it outside and wrapped it around my neck to see how warm it was. It happened to be one of those December days, rare in Idaho, when the sun was actually shining, but it was cold, down near zero. The scarf felt pretty good. I thought Momma would like it. As I took it off and folded it up, it took on a stiff, shiny look like I'd woven it out of aluminum wires. When I looked at it up close though, all I could see was regular Red Heart yarn, fat and a little bit fuzzy. I moved it in and out a few times trying to figure out why it looked so different from far away and up close, but at the time, I couldn't make out anything unusual. Later, I found out that's what dreams always look like when you weave them. They're never the same from two different vantage points.

But at this time, I didn't know anything about dream weaving. I just took the scarf back into the house and wrapped it in a paper grocery sack that I cut and laid flat on the kitchen table. Then I took the leftover yarn and made a bow out of it. I put it under the tree along with the Matchbox car I'd bought for Danny. There were two other presents already there. Those were from Danny to me and Momma. He'd wrapped his in real Christmas paper that Momma saved from when Aunt Doris sent her a present in the mail last year. The paper was printed with little Christmas lights in red and green, and it had 'Merry Christmas!' printed on it in gold letters. I thought it looked real festive. But my bow was better. His bows were just made out of old twine.

Momma always said Christmas was too commercialized; she didn't approve of turning the Christ Child's birthday into an excuse to waste money. But she let us celebrate anyway as long as we didn't go overboard. Not that we could afford to do that. She'd cut a little tree down out of the back field, some scrubby little pine with gaps where there were branches missing, and let Danny and me decorate it with construction paper ornaments and popcorn strings. Across the front, she draped letters cut out of tinfoil that said "Happy Birthday Jesus" instead of "Merry Christmas". And before we opened our gifts, we had a story from the Bible and a prayer.

We put the tree up by the front window, as far away from the woodstove as we could get. Momma didn't want to celebrate Christmas by burning the house down, she said. On Christmas Eve, after we came home from church, Danny and I would rattle our presents from each other and try to guess what they were. We always knew, but we'd always guess something outlandish to make it seem like they were a surprise.

"It looks like a box of erasers," Danny would say, shaking the Matchbox car and looking curious like he didn't get the same darn thing from me every Christmas and birthday of the year.

"It looks like a dead rat," I'd say, squeezing the roll of socks he always put under the tree for me.

"I don't know why you're bothering to guess," Momma would say. "Nobody's getting anything but coal this year. The way you two behaved at Christmas Eve service. I thought Mrs. Colitch was going to have a stroke."

"Oh Momma, Mrs. Colitch always looks like that." And Danny made a Mrs. Colitch face at me, but he was so much shorter that in order to look down his nose, he had to tip his head so far back he almost fell over.

"It's hard to sit still on Christmas," he said. And to prove it, we both jumped up and down chanting "Jingle Bells, Jingle Bells, Jingle Jingle Jingle Jingle," stomping on the floor with each "Jingle."

"You children go to bed," Momma said. "Quit your nonsense. Sairy, make sure your brother brushes his teeth."

14

We never knew when Momma put her presents under the tree. We knew it was Momma, though, and not Santa Claus because Momma didn't hold with secular Christmas traditions, and she told us when we were babies there was no such thing as Santa Claus. In the morning, we'd stay in bed until the sun came up. It was the only day of the year Momma didn't make me get up when she did. We'd lay in bed upstairs and listen to the 'whack!' of her chopping kindling, then hear the draft scrape open, the creak of the stove door and 'thump! Thump!' as she loaded in the wood. After a while, it'd start to warm up, and we'd start punching each other and giggling, throwing our blankets on the floor and wondering what Momma was giving us.

Then, the aroma of sweet rolls would drift upstairs and we would know it was just about time to get up. On Christmas Eve, Momma made a special batch of bread dough, which she rolled up with brown sugar and raisins, and some years, walnuts. She set it down in a cold corner to raise slowly all night, and as soon as the oven heated up, she'd bake those sweet rolls for Christmas breakfast.

It was the one day of the year, also, that Danny wasn't picky about breakfast. Boy, he could wolf down those sweet rolls! They'd come out of the oven simmering in a bath of deep brown caramel goo. We'd eat all the soft rolls from the far side, the colder side, of the oven first, and then eat the ones that were crispy on top from sitting right next to the firebox. One Christmas morning, as I swiped the brown sugar syrup off my plate with one finger, I sang out "Lord Jesus, I wish we could have sweet rolls every day. Thank you God, for your birthday." And Momma glared at me for sacrilege. Momma never raised a hand to punish me. She would just look at me with a stern glance that said "watch it, young lady," and I knew I'd backslid again. It was hard work trying to earn Momma's love.

After breakfast, when I'd done the dishes (there were some chores that didn't get canceled for Christmas), we'd sit down and open our presents. The year I gave Momma the scarf, she gave me a new dress she'd sewed out of thin, shiny fabric with little purple and yellow flowers all over it. I was with her when she bought it at the second-hand store. She was about to put it back, thought it was too thin to be practical, but I loved the slinky feeling of it. I imagined it was real silk, and I badgered her to get it. Well, she'd gotten it, and cut it down into a Christmas dress for me. I stroked the smooth fabric against my cheek and imagined I was Cinderella in the ballroom waiting for my Prince Charming.

She gave Danny a box of school stuff: ruler, pencils, and even a miniature stapler with a box of itty-bitty staples that really worked. I envied him that stapler. He carried it around all morning, stapling together the paper the Christmas presents had been wrapped in until Momma told him he better not use up all his staples because she wasn't buying him any more.

"Now, Momma," I cried, "open *your* presents!"

Momma opened Danny's gift first. It was a tin ring from the dime store, painted gold. It didn't fit on any of her fingers, but she slipped it halfway over one knuckle and oooed and aaaahed over it like it was real gold and diamonds. Then, she opened mine.

"It's beautiful Sairy," she said, and wrapped it around her neck. She tucked in the too-short ends so it wouldn't fall off. When she put it on, it seemed to transform from a misshapen snarl of cheap yarn into a web of translucent glass glistening on her shoulders like sunlight playing on water.

"I wove it for you, Momma," I said.

"I know you did, sweetheart. It's the most beautiful scarf in the whole, wide world." Then she smoothed down my dark hair and kissed me on the forehead. Well! I thought I would float right off the floor, just like those children in the Mary Poppins book who got laughing gas and had a tea party on the ceiling.

# Chapter 2

## ❦ Cate ❧

It was that same year, after Christmas, that I first met Cate. She came to my school in the middle of the year; her family moved up from Boise. No one would've thought we could become best friends. We seemed to be complete opposites. She was a bright, laughing girl with golden hair and deep green eyes, as ethereal as sunshine, and I was melancholy and introverted with dark, lank hair and eyes the color of mud.

The other kids seemed to gravitate toward her right away, clustering around her like puppies vying for attention. She could've joined right in with their hopscotch and four square, but instead, during that first recess, she drifted around the edges of the games, saying "no, thanks" to all the invitations, until she reached me, plodding around the school yard as I always did.

"Hi," she said.

"Hi," I said back.

"I'm Cate. Who're you?"

"I'm Sairy."

She wore a pretty, store-bought dress, with her shiny blond hair falling in silky curls below her shoulders. I hugged my hand-me-down women's jacket tighter around the new dress Momma'd made me for Christmas and just stared at her.

"We're new in town," she said.

"Where'd you-all come from?"

"Boise."

"You got any sisters and brothers?"

"No. It's just me and Mama and Daddy."

"That sounds nice. I have a brother. He's younger than me, and he's spoiled rotten."

17

"Don't you like to play hopscotch?" she said, glancing at the girls clustered together on the pavement.

"It's okay, I guess," I said. "I don't play much, though."

I didn't want to explain that nobody'd play with me. Just one look at Cate and I loved everything about her. She was everything I wanted to be: beautiful, glowing, happy. I was afraid I'd run her off if she knew no one else liked me. She didn't seem worried about it, though. She just fell in beside me like we'd been friends forever, and we walked around the yard together.

"What'd you get for Christmas?" she asked.

"This dress," I said, opening the jacket so she could see it.

"It's nice," she said.

"What'd you get?"

"A new baby doll. You got any baby dolls?"

Momma'd made me a rag doll once, years ago. I took her everywhere with me for a while. I hauled her into the woods and sat her under a tree as I waded through the creek. I made mud-pies with her and decorated her with autumn leaves and cones from the Tamarack trees. By this time, though, I'd worn her down to such a filthy, threadbare condition that all her yarn hair was off and you could barely make out she'd had a face embroidered on with left-over yarn once. I couldn't show that old dirty mess to someone that had a brand new baby doll, so I said no, I didn't have any baby dolls.

"You could borrow one of mine," she offered. I said that sounded fine to me.

"Where do you live?"

"Up north of town a ways."

"Can I come over and see your house? I'll bring some of my dolls. We can play."

Well, this made me nervous. I couldn't imagine someone so pretty hanging around at my house, with its rough log walls and outdoor privy. But she seemed eager to come over, so I said I guessed that would be okay.

That afternoon, she rode the bus home with me.

"Won't your Momma be mad?" I said.

"Nah. She won't care. I'll call her."

"You can't call her from our place," I said, blushing. "We don't have a phone."

"That's okay," she said. "I'll call from school."

I'd never have asked the office to use the phone. It made my heart race and my palms sweat to even walk into the office. It was full of secretaries that looked like they didn't want to be bothered with little girls, but Cate seemed to feel no fear. She just marched right up to the counter that blocked off the outside of the office, where the students and parents had to stand, from all the desks and cupboards where the secretaries sat, and said "I need to use the phone to call my Mama."

"Don't you touch anything else back here," the lady warned that opened the half-door in the counter to let her back. "You kids aren't supposed to be back here.

Cate said "Yes, ma'am," but she turned and made a horrible face at me over her shoulder, rolling her eyes, stretching her mouth in a leer and letting her tongue sag out the side...I started giggling. The secretary that was escorting Cate turned and gave me a dirty look, so I stopped giggling and stared meekly at the floor.

Cate gave her the number, and the secretary talked to the operator.

"That phone hasn't been hooked up yet," she told Cate.

"Here, I'll talk to her," Cate said, taking the phone out of her hand. "Get me the neighbor, then," she told the operator. "We just moved in on Twiney Creek Road next to the Gardiners." Then, a minute later, "Hello, Mrs. Gardiner. This is Cate Johnson.

We just moved in next door. If my Mama wants to know where I am, would you tell her I went home with my friend? Her name is Sairy...." she looked at me, and I said "Perdy." "Sairy Perdy," she said. "Tell her I went to Sairy Perdy's house. No, she doesn't have a phone. I'm calling from school. No, she won't worry. Thank you, ma'am."

We sat together on the bus. I was worried that Danny would fuss about me not sitting with him, but he huddled quietly on the seat right in front of us and fiddled with his schoolbooks. When I saw he wasn't going to cause trouble, then I started worrying about what Cate would think of our house, being used to a nice place in town and a phone and all. Meanwhile, Cate chattered away about how different it was here than down in Boise.

When we got off the bus, she looked around for our house. "It's up the road a ways," I explained. The road, dirt in those days, climbed up a short hill, and then our driveway took off from the right side and wound up a steeper grade. By the time we reached the house, we were puffing a little, but not too much for Cate to take in the rough little cabin, the porch stacked with cordwood up to the roof, and the privy standing at the side, handy to the kitchen door.

"Is this your house?"

"Yes."

"Wow. It's so little."

I guess she must've seen my embarrassment, because she quickly added, "I mean, it's cute."

If the bus hadn't left already, I would have gladly run back down the hill and gotten on, to be delivered anywhere in the wide world except this house, with this girl, so ill-suited to our rough, country life. Dying of starvation or cold seemed a blessing in comparison with Cate's contempt – or pity.

"I guess so," I mumbled.

"Well, c'mon. Let's go in. I want to see the rest."

I saw the house anew as I showed it to Cate. The unpainted wood of the walls and floors soaked up the sunlight filtering in through the pines, giving the place a dark, cozy feel like a ship's cabin. We had no closets. We kept everything neatly organized on open shelves, our whole life out in the open. I keep my house the same way now...nothing hidden. Anyone wants to know what happens in this house, just walk in and look at what's there.

There were sad irons sitting on a marble-top table over by the stove, handy for Momma to reach over and put them on the stove to warm, and one handle for both irons hanging on a hook behind the table. There were jars of home-canned produce on a set of shallow, floor-to-ceiling shelves on the wall near the table, a lidded water barrel standing beside the sink, and Momma's sewing corner taking up half the living room. The kitchen table encroached into the living room, and served as preparation space as well as for eating. There were four chairs around it, two handmade by my Daddy years ago when I was a baby, and each of the remaining ones different than the other, as Momma had collected them from friends at church who didn't need them any more.

Upstairs was Danny's and my room. Its two beds were covered with faded, handmade quilts. Along one wall were a set of shelves and some hooks for our clothes, and we kept our few, battered toys in wooden crates at the foot of each bed. Everything was sturdy, practical, but a little bit makeshift, things re-purposed and used for other things instead of buying new. Cate soaked it in with a bright, inquiring gaze. She plopped down on my bed and looked over at the window that was over Danny's bed.

"How come Danny gets the window?"

I shrugged. "I get up earlier. My bed's closer to the stairs."

21

When Virgil built our place, the place I live in now, he made sure I had a window, two glass doors, actually, that were supposed to open onto a high porch, only the porch never got finished. On summer mornings, when the sun comes up at 4:00, I throw the doors open and watch the light creep over the mountains in the distance. My window looks south, to let the light in. But Danny's window looked north over the draw where the birch and aspen trees grow. When the aspens are in full leaf, even the tiniest breeze makes them dance and the whole draw seems alive with shimmering motion.

"You're lucky," Cate said. "It's pretty up here."

"You wouldn't say that if you had to go to the privy in the snow."

"Privy," she repeated, wrinkling her nose. "Why don't you have a real bathroom?"

"We have a bathroom," I said. "It's only for baths." And I showed it to her, the tiny, windowless room behind the kitchen stove with its cast-iron tub standing on four feet in the middle. One of the feet had fallen off, that's how Momma got it for free from one of the neighbors, who was using it for a feeding trough. Momma set a round piece of tamarack under the corner where the leg was missing and scoured out the dirt that had accumulated over the years that it stood in the neighbor's field, and that's where we bathed.

"How do you fill it up?" she asked, seeing there was no faucet.

"We bring buckets from the stove."

Cate nodded.

"It's a lot of work," I said.

"It's different," she said. "But I like it."

Momma came in from the chicken yard, where she'd been mending a bit of fence to keep the dogs and weasels out of the coop.

"Hello, young lady," she said.

"Hello, ma'am. I'm Cate Stanley."

"One of Sairy's friends from school?"

"Yes, ma'am. We just moved into town."

"Well, that's fine. Sairy, where are your manners? Hang up your guest's coat and see if she'd like a cookie."

"I'm going to take Cate outside, Momma," I said.

I showed Cate all Danny's and my favorite places to play. There were many of these: the pole barn stacked with musty hay bales where we competed to see who could jump off the highest bale, the pond which, this time of year, was nothing but a half-frozen, muddy hole, and the birch grove in the draw.

The birch grove was my favorite place. It became Cate's, too. It was hard to find your way into at any time of year. In the winter, the snow lay in heavy drifts under the dead trees, and you got wet up to your waist clambering through them. In the spring and summer, it was thick with brush that tore your dress or, if you held your skirt out of the way, the skin of your legs. Once you fought your way in, though, under and over fallen, rotting trunks and past the snarl of blackberry vines, you found its secret heart, where a tiny spring welled up into a clear pool. Danny and I had tromped out a small clearing around this, and spent many an hour chasing squeaking toads, floating tiny boats made of bracken, and acting out Bible stories, which were the stories we mostly knew. The spring was barely visible at this time of year, covered with a thick skin of ice and snow, and the draw was quiet and remote, the house invisible through the jumble of papery birch trees.

"I like it back here," Cate said. "You can be all alone whenever you want. I bet nobody bothers you back here."

"Not much," I said. "Momma hollers for us sometimes, and then we have to go. But nobody comes here except Danny and me."

"If I lived in a place like this, I'd stay right here no matter who called."

"You don't know Momma," I said.

"Is she mean to you?"

I found this question bewildering. Why would Momma be mean to me, apart from the usual way of making me do things I didn't much like, such as chores and all?

"No. But she says it's her duty as a Christian woman to raise her children up under proper discipline."

"Does she spank you?"

"No. But still. We have to obey her; that's what the Bible says."

"The Bible? Are you-all churchgoing people?"

"Of course. We're Nazarenes. Don't you go to church?"

"No," Cate said.

I didn't tell Cate, but her answer was a wonderment to me. Of course, I knew there were people who didn't go to church, who didn't believe in God, even. But I'd never met any. I had some idea they were all over in Africa or India or some place far away where the missionaries went.

"Better not tell Momma," I suggested. "Maybe she wouldn't like it."

"We could bring our dolls back here," she said. "In the summer, we could make them go swimming in the spring."

And that's what we did. True to her word, Cate brought some of her dolls up to my place, even left a couple of them there, bedded down in my orange crate, and we'd take them back to the spring and play. Cate could have made friends with any of the town girls. I don't know why she favored me instead, especially after she heard the other kids taunting me about my country ways and hand-me-down clothes. She didn't seem to want to have anything to do with them. She'd stick up for me, even, giving them back insult for insult, and spent her recesses at the back of the school-yard with me, ignoring their games.

She came to my house almost every day. It surprised me that Momma didn't kick up more of a fuss about me having company all the time, especially when we spent so much of the afternoon playing instead of working. Rather than flattening her mouth at me in disapproval, though, when Cate came over for the third or fourth time in a week, she just sat her down at the table with Danny and me for a cookie and some milk, and asked about her day at school like she was part of the family.

Sometimes I thought she almost pitied Cate. Once, when Cate stayed to supper and her Daddy drove over in the car to pick her up afterward, Momma tsk tsked under her breath as she stood on the porch to wave them politely goodbye. She didn't know I was standing behind her listening.

"Why'd you say 'tsk tsk', Momma?" I asked.

I saw a little pucker of concern on her face when she turned around and saw me. "Never mind, Sairy," she said.

I never caught Momma tsk tsking over Cate again, but I couldn't shake the idea that she felt sorry for her. She absorbed her into the normal flow of our family life, included her right along with me in the various projects we always did – baking cookies, darning socks, cutting paper dolls, and sewing handkerchiefs for the missionaries overseas.

"What do the missionaries do with all these handkerchiefs, Mrs. Perdy?" Cate asked.

"They give them to the aborigines, child."

"But why do the aborigines need handkerchiefs? They don't even wear anything, my Daddy says. He says they go around buck neckid."

Momma flattened her mouth at Cate. "In this house, we talk like ladies and gentlemen, dear" she chided her. "The poor aborigines don't have anything, not even the knowledge of Jesus. When we send them these handkerchiefs, we also send them Jesus' love."

I could see Cate wanted to ask more questions about the handkerchiefs and naked aborigines and Jesus' love, but she went back to hemming her handkerchief instead.

Momma seemed to change after that Christmas I gave her the scarf. Sometimes, after I'd scrubbed the floor or straightened up the closet under the stairs, she'd say, "Thank you, Sairy. Why don't you go on outside and play now before supper?" That wasn't like Momma. She hadn't ever seemed to notice when a person needed a break from chores before. Momma worked hard all day, and into the evening, too, and she figured everyone else should do the same.

Some mornings, when she had time, this new Momma would brush and braid my hair before school, and she did it with gentle fingers, not impatient, moving slowly through my hair like a sweet caress and tying each braid up with a bit of yarn in some pretty color. I felt like I mattered to her. And through it all, my scarf hung around her neck. She wore it constantly, even to church. When she took it off to wash it, it still looked dingy and lumpy, but when she wore it, it was smooth, perfect, and glowing with light. Once, I caught her admiring herself in the mirror, turning this way and that to look at the scarf from different angles.

Cate had noticed Momma's scarf right away. "Look how pretty!" she exclaimed, and reached out a finger to trace its translucent-looking threads. Momma's face glowed when she told Cate I'd made it for her, and seeing Momma so pleased over something I'd done made me swell up with pride. I hid it, though. Momma didn't hold with pride because it's against the Bible. I figured I didn't have so much to feel proud about that it wouldn't be okay to indulge for just a minute as long as I kept it to myself.

***

It was in church that I first heard about dream weaving. As I said, Momma wore her scarf there every week. In the dusty gloom of the church, it took on a dark, liquid look like the surface of a deep river at twilight. The ladies there all oohed and aahed over it and said, "How pretty, Ida. Your Sairy made that for you? Well, isn't that fine."

Old Mrs. Moffat, though, she looked at it real close, and rubbed it between her fingers and thumb. Old Mrs. Moffat was a Sunday School teacher we thought must be a hundred or so, and we were all scared of her because her nose was big and knobby and her hair all scraggly like a witch. She was stern, too. When Mrs. Moffat started slapping the table and preaching about the fear of the Lord, which she did often, even the squirmiest boys would sit meekly in their chairs and look at the floor and say "Yes, Ma'am."

I don't know if it was the fear of the Lord we were feeling or the fear of old Mrs. Moffat, but her class was always the best behaved whenever the Sunday School had to stand in front of the church and recite Bible verses from memory. No one cut up or made faces, and if we didn't know the verses, we said them anyway, following the kids who did about half a word behind so she wouldn't know.

I was always one of the ones half a word behind because Mrs. Moffat scared the Bible verses right out of my head, although I could practice them in front of Momma without missing a single "thee" or "thou". To take away some of our awe, we kids called her Mrs. Muffet behind her back because she looked like a big, old spider and was twice as ornery.

After she got a good look at the scarf, she smiled real nice at Momma and said, "Ida, Sairy and me need to have a little conversation in the Sunday School room. Excuse us for a moment, would you?" She grabbed me by the arm and hustled me into the little kids' Sunday School room and closed the door. She sat me down in a little, bitty chair and then sat down herself in the teacher's chair so I could look straight at her knees while she towered over me like the wheels in Ezekiel.

"Now, young lady," she said. "You tell me, what is all this weaving business?"

"It's just something I like to do."

"Who taught you to weave like that?"

"Nobody. I learned it out of a book." Then, I dared to look up past her knees to her face and ask, "What's wrong with it?"

"There's nothing wrong with weaving, child," she said. "So long as it's done with the fear of the Lord. Do you fear the Lord?"

"Yes, ma'am."

We sat silently for a moment, and Mrs. Moffat stopped glaring at me and began staring out the window.

"My Granny used to weave like that," she said absently. "My Granny was a God-fearing woman. She was a dream-weaver and a God-fearing woman."

"What's a dream-weaver?"

Mrs. Moffat stopped looking out the window and looked at me sternly. "Never you mind," she said. "The less said about it, the better. My Granny told me she wouldn't teach me, or anyone, how to weave dreams. It's dangerous business, she said, trying to meddle with the Lord's will. Sairy, you wouldn't try to meddle with God's will, now, would you?"

"No, ma'am."

"Well, I think you can find better things to do with your time than this silly weaving. Don't think I didn't notice you pretending to know your Bible verses last week during recitation, young lady. You should spend your time learning your Bible instead of mooning around over the loom."

"I know my Bible verses, ma'am. Honest. I just get nervous and they kind of fly out of my head. Besides, Momma doesn't see anything wrong with weaving. She says it's good I'm doing something productive."

"Your Momma is a good woman. Even if she does spoil you children. But you mark what I say, Sairy Perdy. Dream weaving is dangerous business."

Mrs. Moffat was the only person that ever talked to me about dream-weaving. She's the only one I ever met who'd known a dream-weaver besides me. And that's all she told me. I had to learn the rest on my own.

# Chapter 3

## ❧ The Headband ❧

After Cate met Momma, she wanted to know everything about her. Once, when Momma was at church with the Nazarene Ladies' Circle, she talked me into sneaking into Momma's room and looking through her things – clothes and hairbrushes and makeup and such. Of course, Momma didn't wear real makeup. But she had lavender-scented powder and some lotion for her face. Cate ran her fingers across the powder puff, feeling its softness, and then dabbed a bit of powder under her nose so she could smell the lavender. She brushed her hair with Momma's hairbrush. She went through her jewelry box and held up the pair of earrings Momma got from her Granny, pretending she was wearing them and admiring how they looked in the mirror.

She asked me what Momma's real name was and how old she was. And she asked me about Daddy.

"My Daddy's dead," I said. "He died when Danny was a baby."

"How'd he die?" she wanted to know.

"He got hit by a train one night," I said.

I barely remember my Daddy. I was barely more than two when he died. Momma has a picture of him in her bedroom, and that's the way I remember him...dark haired, mustache, dark eyes hooded and full of mystery. I have a memory of clinging to his leg while he jounced me up and down, but I might've made that up.

Cate thought I was lucky to have only a Momma. "Just you and your Momma and your brother," she said. "I wish I had only a Momma. Even if I had to share her with my brother."

"Don't you like your Daddy?" I said, puzzled. I'd always wondered whether things wouldn't have been better if Daddy hadn't've died. Maybe we'd have indoor plumbing, for instance.

Cate didn't answer me. She just started playing with Momma's jewelry, draping a string of pearls around her neck and holding up a pin against the collar of her dress.

"We have to put it back," I said. "Momma'll be mad if she finds out we were messing with her jewelry."

"Okay," she said, and started putting everything away just so. Cate was like that back then. She didn't enjoy getting a person in trouble. When I told her Momma wouldn't allow something, she didn't press me to do it. Toward other adults, she was more defiant. She hid it, though, and was naughty behind their backs while saying respectful "yes, ma'ams" and "yes, sirs" to their faces.

She picked up the picture of Daddy and Momma that Momma left sitting on her dressing table. "Is this your Daddy?" she said.

"Yes," I said. In the picture, Daddy and Momma looked serious, like two judges staring at a condemned prisoner. Daddy stood a little behind Momma and rested his hand on her shoulder. Had they loved each other? A child doesn't know things like that.

"Was he nice?" Cate asked.

"I think so," I said cautiously. "I don't remember him too well."

*** 

Cate and I spent most of our time outside when the weather wasn't too cold. We took Cate's dolls out to the spring and made up stories about them. They had a family – a wicked stepmother and several bratty sisters. Our favorite dolls were the heroines: sweet, gentle and always getting picked on. They'd run away from home and have adventures in the wilderness, build shelters out of sticks and cook over a campfire. The campfires were real, tiny fires built out of little twigs and dry birch leaves. Good thing Momma never found out we were building fires. Heaven knows what she would've done about it, maybe assigned me to hoe weeds for a year for threatening to start a forest fire.

When we got tired of those games, Cate would tell me stories from the movies. Momma didn't take us to the movies. I don't know if it was because she didn't think they were scriptural or just because they were a waste of time. Cate went to the movies all the time, and she would enthrall me with magic tales of characters whose wealth and sophistication I could hardly imagine. She remembered every detail of the stories, and acted them out as she told them, smoking an invisible cigarette and looking down her nose as she drawled 'daahling', or casting herself tearfully on the bosom of a tree, which stood in for the hero. After she'd told me a movie a couple of times so I knew the story as well as she did, we'd act it out together, using Cate's dolls for the characters.

During the coldest part of winter, we had to stay in the house. Instead of wilderness escapades, the dolls had cinematic adventures. We wrapped them up in the fanciest scraps we could find from Momma's fabric box and pretended they were going to cocktail parties. Since Cate didn't have any boy dolls, the men were absent, but the girls would smoke and talk about them so they seemed just as real as if they'd been there. If it'd just been me, Momma wouldn't have approved of smoking, even pretend, but she didn't fuss so much when Cate was around. Only if we giggled too loud or started running around the house would she say, "Girls, mind your manners. This is a civilized house, and you're acting like a couple of barnyard animals."

Danny hung around on the fringes of our games, but we usually wouldn't let him play.

"Go hang out with your cub scout friends," I'd order, and we would run deeper into the woods, hiding from him and climbing higher in the trees than he could go, tossing twigs down at him from above and taunting him as a girly boy and a crybaby. He'd run to Momma and tattle on us, and Momma would come out on the porch and holler, "You two let your little brother play!"

So then we would make him play all the boring parts in our stories: the evil stepparents, or even more often, the dog. Danny just wasn't cut out to be the evil stepparents. His wickedness was lackluster; he would simply order us to clean our rooms or dust the furniture. He had no capacity for real meanness.

Strange how my memories of Cate are more real to me than those of Danny. He had an air of impermanence even then, an inability to make his presence felt. He was just the bothersome little brother we were forced to accommodate when we couldn't hide quick enough to avoid him.

One day, scrambling to keep ahead of him, we led him through the draw and up the hill behind it onto the 80 acres in back of Momma's place where nobody lived. We'd step on a dead branch every so often, or giggle, and he ran after us until he was far out of sight from the house in a place he'd never been. Then, we left him there and ran back, careful to keep quiet so he couldn't follow. Dark started to fall, and still he hadn't found his way back. I got worried at that and wanted to go looking for him, but Cate complained that he'd tell Momma and we'd get in trouble.

"He'll tell anyway," I said. "Besides, he'll be afraid up there in the dark by himself." I made her come with me, and we tramped back up the hill, calling for him. He'd wandered in the direction opposite to home. We found him tearstained, huddled under a fir tree, trembling with fright. I was overcome with remorse. I dropped to my knees and cradled him, petted away his tears and told him I was sorry.

33

But Cate made him promise not to tell or we wouldn't take him back with us and he could just spend the night there in the woods. So we told Momma we'd all gotten lost and Danny'd been separated from us accidentally.

Momma was still cross because we'd wandered too far off, and she curtailed our explorations, saying we weren't to cross the fence of our own property again. We paid no mind to this, and rambled as far as we had time to do and still get back before supper, but only when Danny was at scouts or doing homework.

***

One day, shortly before the end of the year, Cate came to school with an ugly bruise on her arm.

"You've got a bruise on your arm," I said.

"I know."

"That's a big one. How'd it happen?" I examined the bruise more closely. There was a big, black spot with a few littler spots on one side.

"My Daddy gave it to me," she said.

"Your Daddy," I said, not understanding. "Your Daddy gave you an accident?"

"No," she said. "He gave it to me on purpose."

"How'd your Daddy give you a bruise?"

"He hit me."

"Your Daddy hit you on purpose?" This idea was completely foreign to me. Momma might be stern, and she might be hard to please, but never had she ever struck me.

"He hits me all the time," she said.

"Well, how come he does that?"

"He's just mean, is all. He even hits Mama."

"You-all must be doing something wrong. Your Daddy wouldn't hit you for no reason."

"Mama says it's because he's drunk," she said.

"You mean, your Daddy drinks alcohol?" I was shocked. I knew drinking alcohol was a sin. "Momma says it's against the Bible to drink alcohol."

"I don't think Daddy believes in the Bible," she said. "Or if he does, he doesn't care what's in it, because he drinks alcohol all the time. Then he gets mad and starts whipping on Mama and me."

Well, I had to get more information about this. It'd never occurred to me that people might beat on their own family. So I made haste to relate the whole thing to Momma.

"That poor child," she said. "I thought it might be something like that."

"Momma, her daddy's drinking alcohol. Isn't that against the Bible?"

"Honey, folks do things against the Bible all the time. That's the problem with this world. And now you can see what happens when they do...they start doing all kinds of other bad things, too, like hitting their children."

"Shouldn't – shouldn't we do something about it, Momma? Shouldn't we do something to stop it?"

"I don't like it, child, but it's not our place to interfere between a man and his family."

"Well, why can't she come live with us, then? We could take her in."

"It doesn't work that way," Momma shook her head. "You can't just take a child away from her parents. The law wouldn't permit it."

This didn't make sense to me. Why would the law be on the wrong side? But Momma said there was nothing to be done, so that's the way it was.

After that, Cate showed me bruises frequently. Mostly, they were hidden under her clothes, on her legs, or she'd wear long sleeves.

"Why don't you run away?" I asked. "Why don't you run outside and hide?"

"I can't," she said. "He's faster than me, and I'd catch hell for trying to run."

"You shouldn't say 'catch hell', Cate. It's like swearing."

"That's what my Mama calls it," she said. "'Cate, you'll catch hell for that when your Daddy gets home.' Sometimes she even tells on me."

The thought of Cate's daddy beating up on her upset me, but Cate seemed to accept it. Over time, I got used to her showing up with marks and stopped paying attention to it.

*** 

That year, for the first time in my life, Momma let me have a birthday party. Of course, there was no one there but Cate, Momma and Danny, but it was a party just the same. She made me a cake, and Cate got to spend the whole night. As sweet as that cake was, it was sweeter still to think that Momma made a birthday party just for me. We sat around the table and they sang 'Happy Birthday, dear Sairy', and I thought my heart would burst out of my chest – I was the most special girl on the planet.

I gave Cate my bed that night, and I slept on the floor. We stayed awake half the night, giggling and telling stories until Danny whined to Momma that we were waking him up, and then she told us to stop carrying on and go to sleep. Cate wouldn't say another word after that. She'd do anything to keep Momma from being mad at her. She kept her naughtiness for other people.

Cate and I were best friends. I told her everything, even how Momma liked Danny better than me until I gave her the scarf. Cate seemed struck by that. She asked me about it over and over again, how Momma was before and how she was after, trying to figure out what made her change her mind. She kept looking at the scarf, too, which seemed to get more beautiful over time. It took on sort of an incandescent glow that lit up Momma's face in the dark. It got so you couldn't really tell what color it was...the colors just chased each other across the surface of the scarf like the iridescent colors on a soap bubble.

Cate was so fascinated by it that I even told her about Mrs. Moffat and her granny, the dream-weaver.

"What's a dream-weaver?" she said.

"I don't know. Mrs. Moffat wouldn't tell me."

"Does that mean you can do anything you want to? Just by weaving it?"

"I don't know." Then I reminded her, "Mrs. Moffat said it was dangerous to meddle with God's will."

"Oh, pooh. What does Mrs. Moffat know? My Mama and Daddy don't even believe in God."

"Don't believe in God?" I was shocked. "How can they not believe in God?"

"I don't know, but they don't. So maybe dream-weaving means you can do magic."

"Magic is wicked. Momma says it's sorcery, and the Bible is against sorcery."

"Well," Cate said reasonably, "if there's no God, then how can magic be wicked?"

"There is a God," I said.

"How do you know?"

"I just know. And weaving is not magic."

*** 

Whether my weaving was magic or not, I loved the process of it. I loved the feeling that I could be competent at something, and that I could make something pretty out of nothing more than a ball of thread. I was determined to improve. So, I figured I'd use those leftover scraps of Red Heart to weave something else, something for Cate. I didn't have much left, so it'd have to be something small, maybe a headband. I would've liked to surprise her, but she was over at our house so often it was hard to keep it secret. So I went ahead and told her what I was doing.

Cate entered into the idea enthusiastically. Before I started, I told her, we had to find something better for the loom than the twisted old sticks I'd picked up in the woods. . They made the warps slide around, getting looser or tighter depending on whether they hit a dip or a bump, and I needed them to be uniform. So we scouted around for something more even, finally finding an old broomstick in the pole barn, which I cut in half. For all the rest, the heddle sticks and such, my old sticks would work even if they weren't perfect.

Cate watched me measure out the warps and slip them onto the top and bottom sticks of the loom. She watched me weave two sticks in at top and bottom, one in each shed, to hold the warps an even distance apart. She watched me weave the heddle stick into one shed, then make the string heddles and loop them over the other heddle stick. None of this took very long because the piece was so narrow. In a couple of hours, I was ready to weave. I tied the top stick to one of the posts holding up the second floor, where Danny's and my bedroom was, and then I tied my strap to the bottom stick so I could stretch the warps tight between my body and the post.

"What color do you want?" I asked Cate, indicating the pile of Red Heart scraps.

"That one," she said, pointing to the dark green.

Since I had no bobbins or shuttles, I wound the weft around a small stick, and began to weave. For a beater, I used an old comb of Mommas. It came down from Granny, I think, a fancy plastic comb that an old-fashioned lady might stick in her hair for decoration.

Cate watched every pass of the shuttle intently.

"Is this going to be magic?"

"No, I told you it's not magic."

"I wish it was," she said. "I wish I could come live with you, at your house. I wish you could make that come true."

"Momma says you can't live with us," I said. "She says the law wouldn't allow it. You can't take folks away from their parents."

"Well, then, I wish my daddy would just go away and never come back."

I passed the weft through a couple of sheds. "What would your mama do without him?" I asked. "Wouldn't it be better if he stayed, but was nice to you-all instead of mean?"

At this, a picture rose up in my mind of Cate standing alone, with a high, broad stone wall all the way around her. That wasn't what I'd been thinking of at all. I didn't want Cate behind walls; I wanted her daddy to love her the way Momma loved me. I wanted him to stroke her blond hair and kiss her forehead and call her 'sweetheart'. I commanded my mind to conjure up a picture of that, instead of this lonely wall, but it didn't happen. I learned later on that you have to be careful because once a dream comes, it's set and there's no changing it.

"I think it'd be better if he just left," Cate said.

Every day when we got home from school, Cate would badger me about the headband, so I'd tie on my loom and she'd sit there and chatter while I wove. It didn't take long to finish. I cut it off the loom and tied the ends, then I handed it to Cate. She held it across her palms and rubbed her cheek up and down its length. It was a little better than Momma's scarf, but still far from beautiful. That didn't seem to bother Cate. She handed it back to me and said "Tie it in my hair." So I put it over the top of her head and then tied the ends in back of her neck, under her heavy, blond hair. It bisected that river of gold like a rough-hewn boat cutting through the water.

"I'm going to look in the mirror," she said, running into the bathroom, where Granny's oval, wood-framed mirror hung above the washstand.

"Look!" she said. We stood side-by-side, holding hands and examining her reflection in the mirror. The headband now appeared dark and uncompromising, like a band of steel strapped across her head.

"Do you like it?" I said doubtfully. I'd hoped for something delicate, in keeping with her fragile beauty.

"It's perfect," she said.

She wore the headband every day, same as Momma wore her scarf. I was proud that she liked it so much.

"I feel better with it on," she explained. "I like to imagine I don't really belong to Mama and Daddy. They just found me on a street corner somewhere and stole me. My real family is someone completely else, someone beautiful and rich. That makes me feel brave. Sometimes, I stand right up to Daddy and tell him 'You're not even my real father. I don't have to mind you.'"

"You have to mind your Daddy," I said. "You mustn't say things like that. Don't make him mad."

"Oh, he's just an old drunk," she said.

One day, she came to school excited. She was late, just slipped into her seat before the bell, so I didn't get a chance to talk to her before class. I had to wait until the first recess to hear what'd happened. As soon as our feet hit the playground, she seized my hand and dragged me out to the furthest corner of the yard where nobody could overhear.

"It worked," she said.

"What worked?"

"The headband. It worked. I knew it was magic."

"What do you mean 'it worked'? It's a headband. It's supposed to keep your hair out of your face."

"I don't mean it worked like that," she said. "Daddy got drunk again last night. He got all wound up and started hollering, like usual. Well, with Daddy, hollering leads to hitting, so we all knew what was coming. So Mama made me clear the table while she stayed in the kitchen. Sure enough, Daddy got mad at me for banging the plates around and started yelling at me to stop breaking all the damn plates. So I told him I was clearing the table same as always and the plates were going to be fine. He jumped up out of his chair and said I better stop sassing him or he was going to teach me some manners."

I was agog. "Weren't you scared?"

"No, I wasn't a bit scared. I put my hands on my hips and looked right back at him and said 'You better not touch me.' Then, he pulled back his hand and tried to wallop me across the ear, but his hand kind of bounced back, like. And he bellowed 'Dammit!' like he got hurt. And I couldn't even feel it. It was like his hand ran into a brick wall before he even touched my ear. So I said 'See. I told you you better not.' And Mama came running in from the kitchen saying 'What's going on?' And Daddy said 'I'm disciplining that little brat of yours and she hurt my hand. You better get on back to that kitchen RIGHT NOW.' So Mama left, of course, because she didn't want Daddy to start hitting on her, too. But he didn't, Sairy. He didn't hurt me at all."

I remembered the wall I'd seen in my mind's eye right as I started weaving the headband, and I wondered if it could possibly be the same wall that kept Cate's daddy from knocking her ear off.

"You did it," Cate said. "You saved me. This headband is stronger than Daddy. It's the strongest thing there is." She

41

grabbed my hands and swung them back and forth in huge, joyous arcs. "You're my best friend, forever. I'll always love you best. You can weave anything you want," she said. "You can make things happen."

"But I don't think I can," I protested. "I don't think it has anything to do with what happened. Don't tell anyone else."

*** 

"Momma," I asked Momma that night, "can people make things come true by thinking about them?"

"No, Sairy," she said. "People make things come true by doing something about them. If people could make things happen just by wishing, why half the people in this world would be rich and famous, wouldn't they?"

I guessed Momma was right. The water never hauled itself and the firewood never chopped itself, and all the wishing in the world wasn't going to make it happen.

I told Cate what Momma had said. She thought about it for a while, and then asked me, "Then how do you explain what happened with Daddy? And how do you explain what happened with your Momma, when you made her the scarf? And how do you explain what Mrs. Moffat said about being a dream-weaver?"

I couldn't explain it. So Cate proposed an experiment: sit down and weave something on purpose, she suggested. Think something up, and see if you can make it come true.

"I don't think that's a good idea."

"Come on, Sairy. Don't be such a scaredy-cat. Do it. You want to know, don't you?"

I think I already knew, and that's why I resisted. Cate kept after me, though. She was always persistent about getting her way.

"Make it something good," she said. "That way you don't have to worry about doing anything wrong."

After a couple of weeks of her badgering, I gave in, as I always did. We talked over what I should make and decided I should weave something for Danny. He was sickly, like I said before. He got earaches and colds constantly, and Momma was always fretting about how delicate he was. So I decided to weave him a cap to keep him well.

"Great! Perfect!" Cate approved. "See...magic can be good. You can do good with it and then it's not wicked."

I started it after school let out, and worked on it most of the summer. Cate monitored my progress, as interested as she'd been in the headband, though she didn't fuss at me to work on it every day. "I guess there's no hurry. He's not going to catch cold during the summer," she said.

Right off, I had trouble with it. I'd saved up and bought myself some more Red Heart: a bright, royal blue, Danny's favorite color. The warps didn't seem to want to settle right on the loom; they kept bunching up and getting tangled. And then, the string heddles, which I wound in a continuous thread from one end of the stick to the other, kept changing length so some were too long and others too short, so the shed wouldn't open right and I kept putting the weft over a thread it was supposed to go under. Last, I started breaking warps, which would get frayed by the stick heddle until they wore right through.

I'd planned to conjure up a picture of Danny healthy and strong and keep that in my mind as I wove. But the vision wouldn't come clear. Instead, I spent all my weaving time fuming about the loom not working right. I was too busy knotting together warps, which then would be too short and mess up the tension on all the other warps, and back-tracking to redo pieces where the weft went over and under the wrong warps because of the sheds being wrong. I couldn't keep any picture in mind, and I couldn't relax and get into the rhythm of the weaving. When I thought of Danny, I thought of him as he was, undersized, with a runny nose and protruding, anxious eyes, not sturdy and healthy as I wanted him to be.

I did finish the hat, finally, full of mistakes. There was one warp that didn't get woven into either shed most of the way down; apparently it'd broken and I'd tied it on the wrong side of the stick heddle and left it out of the string heddle. So it made a long, vertical loop up half the length of the hat. I was disgusted with the whole thing and came close to throwing it away, but Momma wouldn't let me. She took out a yarn needle and sewed the warp down to the hat with red yarn. So the hat was blue with a tiny red stripe half way across.   Then she sewed up the sides and we gave it to Danny.

Danny wore it to be nice, because he was a sweet boy, not because he liked it particularly. Momma would snug it firmly down over his ears in the morning, and he'd slip it off and put it in his pocket before we got on the bus, because the first day he wore it some of the other kids made fun of it. Cate and I watched him for weeks to see if he was getting healthier. For a while, we thought maybe he was, because he didn't get an earache for weeks even though he wasn't wearing a hat during autumn chill. But in October, he got the worst cold I'd ever seen, and we had to admit the hat hadn't worked.

"See," I told Cate. "Momma was right. You can't make things happen just by wishing for them."

Actually, I was kind of relieved. I didn't want to be responsible for things happening just because my mind dreamed them up. I didn't want to get in trouble for meddling with God's will, like Mrs. Moffat warned. And I also didn't want to stop weaving. Except for my frustrating experience with the hat, I loved the slow, peaceful process, and the fact that my mind could range free while I kept my hands occupied with something productive, as Momma would say. It was a way I could gather wool without Momma finding me something useful to do.

"Maybe the hat didn't work because you didn't want it bad enough," Cate said. "You didn't really want Danny to be well."

"I did too. I want Danny to be well."

I did. But there's wanting and then there's *wanting*, if you take my meaning.

# Chapter 4

## ❧ Cate's House ❧

It was that fall, after the disappointment of Danny's hat, that I started hounding Cate to take me to her house. I was scared to meet her daddy, a little, but she said he'd never even tried to hit her since that day he smashed his hand trying to box her ear, so she figured maybe he'd learned his lesson. Now, as her mama said, he was busy trying to drink himself to death.

"It's not fair we never go over to your house," I complained. "I don't even know what your room looks like. You know everything about my house. We've played every game practically to death. I want to see where you live for a change."

"There's nothing special about it," she said. "It's just a house like every other house. We don't have a spring, or a pond, or a pole barn. Just a plain, old yard. There's nothing to do there."

"But I want to see it," I said. "I want to see the phone, and the radio."

I wanted to see her Daddy, too. I'd never met a drunk before. I envisioned him with horns sprouting out of his head and fire on his breath, like Satan, himself. Cate said no, he was just an ordinary person, but his face did get a little red when he drank.

She finally gave in, reluctantly, and brought me home one day after school. It was late in the autumn, and an early snow had fallen, then thawed, then frozen again. Her porch steps, unlike ours, which were always neatly swept and scraped, were covered with snow embedded with dozens of footprints. The random ridges and depressions, along with slick patches where the sun hadn't yet melted the ice, made for treacherous footing. The yard was bare except for one bedraggled tree that looked like it might be dead, and the house had some peeling paint on the boards up near the roof.

We dropped our books and coats in the foyer and wiped our feet on a small, dirty rug in front of the door. The house was a lot bigger than Momma's, and brighter, with light-colored paint on the walls, but not nearly as neat. There were a few pieces of stuffed furniture in the living room, a couch and a couple of chairs, and some little tables scattered in between. I couldn't figure out what Cate's family did in that room. The little tables were dusty and had a few magazines on top, and a dirty coffee cup, but except for that, the room didn't look like it was used for anything.

There was a separate room for eating in, with a table and a large, low buffet over by the wall. On top of the buffet were an array of bottles with different colored liquids in them, and a bunch of glasses. You couldn't see into the kitchen, as it was cut off from the other two rooms by a narrow doorway that led off the dining room. At the back of the living room, I saw a dark hall leading to the back of the house, where I guessed the bedrooms must be.

"Hi, Mama," Cate called. "I brought Sairy over."

"Sairy," said a soft, high voice. "Who's that?"

"Sairy, my friend. The girl I go over to see all the time."

"Oh, right. Hi Sairy." A woman appeared at the kitchen doorway. She looked thin and worried, with colorless hair fluffed up around her face like a dust bunny had settled on her head.

"How do you do, ma'am," I said.

I expected Cate's Mama to ask where I lived, and where did I go to church, and who was my Momma, and all the things I was used to grown-ups asking, but she just stared at me for a minute, and said "I'm okay, I guess," before drifting back into the kitchen.

"Mama," Cate said, "can we have a cookie?"

47

"There aren't any cookies left," her Mama said.

"Oh, that's okay," I told Cate. "I'm not hungry. Let's go see your room."

I could hardly imagine what it would be like to have your very own room. Danny and I shared a room because the whole upstairs of our house was only big enough for one room. He slept at one end, under the window, and I slept at the other. When I got mad at him, I put a row of stuff, books and some old dishes Momma gave me to play house with, on the floor down the middle to divide his part from mine.

"This is a wall," I insisted, "and you can't come through it without asking." Since my bed sat beside the top of the stairs, he couldn't get to his part of the room without walking through mine, and instead of asking permission, he'd just whine to Momma that I was being mean to him. My wall of dishes wasn't near as good as a real wall anyway, since all he had to do was look across the room to see exactly what I was doing. It didn't block noise, either, so when Cate and I played up there, Danny was always hanging around trying to join in. I thought it must be heaven to have your own room, and I told Cate so.

"I don't know," she said. "Sharing with Danny's not so bad."

"You say that because you don't have to share with him," I said.

Cate's room had real walls, painted the loveliest pale pink color. There was a fluffy, white rug on the floor beside her bed, and the bed was covered with a dark pink bedspread with white lace all around the edges. The whole thing reminded me of a bowl of marshmallow fluff with bits of peppermint candy sprinkled on top. She had a collection of dolls, not just one or two but a whole raft of them. They sat in a line on top of a shelf, and on the lower shelves were other toys: a tea set, a play cash register, a little blackboard and a box of chalk…there were so many toys I didn't even know where to start playing.

"Just look at all these toys!" I marveled. "What shall we play with first? Let's play grocery store." Cate didn't seem all that excited about playing grocery store, or with any of the toys, for that matter.

"I like it better over at your house," she said.

"Are you crazy? Why, we don't have a thing to play with over there!"

"There's the birch woods, and the field, and the place below the driveway. There's the pole barn and the chicken yard and the pond. There's a hundred things to do there. And your momma doesn't run out of cookies," she said.

I supposed she was right, but as far as I was concerned, I'd rather have a play cash register and a chalkboard and a tea set. After her daddy came home, though, I could see where maybe all those toys weren't enough to make a person want to stay home. He came in late in the afternoon, smelling like Momma's medicine box and bumping clumsily into the doorframe. He propped himself unsteadily against the door for a moment, not coming into the room. He didn't kiss Cate hello. He didn't even look at her, just bellowed "Cassie!" and Cate's mama came out of the kitchen and gave him a nervous peck on the cheek.

"We got any gin?" he said.

"We're out of that," said Cate's mama.

"Well, shit," he said. That shocked me. I wasn't used to hearing people curse. Momma never cursed, and she couldn't abide people who did.

"Who's this?" he said, noticing me and Cate standing in the hallway. "Who're you?"

"I'm Sairy, Mr. Johnson," I said, bobbing a little hint of a curtsey, since that was the greeting Momma expected me to give when meeting adults. I was careful to remember my manners even though he cursed.

"Sairy. You that hick Catie hangs out with all the time?"

This confused me. I wasn't too sure exactly what a hick was.

"I guess so, sir," I said carefully.

"Sairy isn't a hick," Cate flared. "She's my best friend."

"Huh," her father said, scowling at her. "She looks like a hick to me." He lost interest in me and stalked into the living room, stumbling slightly over the throw rug by the door. He threw himself down on the couch and said, "When's supper, Cassie?"

"Don't you sass your father," Cate's mama warned her.

"I'd better be going," I told Cate. I had a long walk home, and I didn't relish finishing up my chores in the cold, dark evening.

\*\*\*

"What's a hick, Momma," I asked later, as we cleared dishes from the table.

"Hick is what ignorant people call folks who don't have a lot of money," she said.

"Are we hicks?"

"I guess so, honey," she said. "We surely don't have a lot of money. But the Lord provides for His own."

After I went to bed that night, I thought about what Momma'd said. Danny was sleeping at the other end of our room, and I could see a little Danny-shaped lump stirring under the worn coverlet as he shifted from side to side, dreaming, maybe, about playing soldier, ducking behind a clump of scrubby pines and peering out from behind to ambush the enemy advancing across the field, shooting them with the stout stick he used as a gun or lobbing a pine-cone grenade. That stick could be a machine

50

gun, a bazooka or a sniper rifle, and had been all of those on various military missions he and I had been part of.

Momma was knitting downstairs, and before I fell asleep, I heard her get up out of her rocking chair and turn off all the lights, click, click, click. She went into the bathroom to brush out her hair and wash her face. I heard her pouring water from the pitcher into the bowl on the washstand and setting the pitcher down with a tinny clunk as the porcelain rang on the marble top of the washstand. Then, she flicked the switch in the bathroom, too, and I heard her bedroom door close. I fell asleep thinking about Cate's loveless house and how the Lord provided for me and Danny and Momma. There were worse things than being hicks.

***

After having such a time with Danny's hat and the broken warps, I made up my mind to get something better than old Red Heart yarn, and I wanted a real shuttle, not the little twigs I was using that kept catching on the warps and pulling threads loose. It took me a long time to save up for those things. I rented myself out to the neighbors for anything they'd pay me to do: shelling peas, hoeing weeds, beating rugs, polishing floors, and even taking care of Mrs. Reed's goats while she was away for a couple weeks visiting her daughter. I didn't buy so much as a cold Coca Cola with the nickels and dimes I earned. Every one of 'em went into the little hoard I was collecting for a shuttle and some real weaving yarn.

When I finally got the shuttle, I couldn't leave it alone. It was smooth and flat and could carry three times as much weft as any of those little twigs. I kept rubbing it between my hands to feel how satiny it was...there wouldn't be any snagging with this! I carried it around with me for days until I almost lost it by dropping it behind the wood shed by accident. Then I put it with all my loom sticks until the yarn came.

The yarn was hard, stiff cotton thread, like my string only wound tighter. The color was deep, royal blue with tiny specks of yellow, red and green twisted all through. Oh, it was beautiful! I'd had months to plan what I was going to do with it. I wanted to weave my Granny a runner to set across the foot of her bed.

Granny was Momma's momma. In those days, she was as gnarly and arthritic as I am now, and she always smelled of liniment that she spread on her knees and ankles to "loosen up her old bones," as she would say. She didn't live in Idaho with us, but over in Kennewick, Washington. She looked a lot like Momma, only looser and knobbier, with dark age spots covering her hands. She and Momma didn't always see eye to eye, and whenever they'd argue, Granny's dark eyes would snap like a green knot in a hot fire, and she'd tell Momma, "Ida, don't you contradict your Momma. 'Honor thy father and mother', the Bible says."

"Momma," Momma would say, "the Bible says I got to honor you, not pretend like you have any sense."

Funny thing was, Momma treated me the same way Granny treated Momma. As far as I could tell, they were two peas in a pod and should've gotten along just fine. I asked Momma about it once, when I got older, and she said, "Sairy, just because we fussed doesn't mean we didn't love each other. I guess we were too much alike to live in the same house for long." Until then, it'd never occurred to me people could be too much alike to get along. Maybe that's why Cate and I were such good friends; we were as different as could be.

Now that I had real weaving yarn, I wanted Granny's runner to be as good as store-bought, so I wove it carefully. With a few pieces under my belt, I knew some of the things that could go wrong, and I was determined to make it pretty. Despite all my efforts, it still went in and out some at the selvedges. It's tricky to make a straight piece on a back-strap loom. Still, it was far and away the nicest thing I'd ever made. As I wove, I thought about Granny and her wispy, white hair pulled back into a tight knot on the back of her head and her fluffy shawl all drawn up tight around her thin chest to keep the cold off her. Granny had to keep the cold off even when it was practically summer and the rest of us were running around barefoot in sleeveless dresses.

Funny thing was, as I wove, that picture of Granny got younger and younger. I saw her wrinkles smooth out, and her eyes, sharp and faded in color like a bleached stone, took on a soft glow and turned yellowish-brown. She stood straight and tall, like Momma, not all hunched over like she really was. The age spots on her hands faded away, and her fingers became long and elegant. I'd never seen Granny when she was young. She looked strong, confident and happy.

I gave Granny the runner when we drove down to see her on Thanksgiving, as we sometimes did. She unfolded it and draped it across her lap to give it a good look.

"Well, Sairy, that's just fine," she said. "You take that in and put it on my bed for me."

So I took it into her bedroom and spread it across the foot of her bed, on top of the old log cabin quilt she'd made right after she married Grampy, when they were both young, long before Grampy died of a tree falling on him. The quilt used to be a bouquet of bright colors, but by now it was faded to washed-out shades of gray and pink and primrose. Grammy'd quilted it by hand, thousands of intricate stitches making elaborate curlicues all over the face of it. The runner drained all the color out of it, a dark slash across its threadbare surface with fringes hanging down almost to the floor. I stood there looking at it for a while, and then I moved it up to the top of the bed, draping it across Granny's pillow instead, where she could lay her head on it.

She told me later that the runner was working out just fine.

"I sleep real peaceful on it, Sairy," she said. "Seems like I just drift on back to the days when your Grampy was with me and we were both young. Those were good days. I like remembering 'em."

"I'm glad you like it, Granny," I said.

***

After I wove Granny's runner, everyone started taking my weaving seriously. It got so I could tell Momma "I'm weaving," and she wouldn't call me away to fetch something. Sometimes Momma would ask me why don't you weave me a set of napkins, or a potholder, or something else for around the house, and I would. She'd give me all the scraps from her knitting, and I wove strips out if them that I sewed together into a throw rug for Danny's and my room. We'd take a running start across the floor, land on that rug and surf across the waxed wood floor until we crashed into Danny's bed.

I still have that rug. Now it sits in front of my door so's people can wipe their feet on it when they're about to track mud into the house. It's a little threadbare, but I can see a dozen sweaters, socks, gloves and hats in it that Momma knit for me and Danny, things that cuddled us up through many snowy winters. I even see a pink stripe where I put leftovers from the sweater she made for Cate. Like Granny said, it contains good memories.

# Chapter 5

## ⊷ Sairy on Her Own ⥳

As the years went by, Cate and I got cemented together like two rocks in a wall. She spent so much time at my house people started to forget we weren't for-real sisters. Every now and then, we'd put in an appearance at her house, but despite all her fancy toys, we didn't have as much fun there as we did at our place.

Her Daddy'd left not too long after I made the headband for her, just walked out of the house one night to go drinking and never came back. Cate never found out if he was dead or alive. She didn't have much to say about it, just shrugged like she was better off without him.

"Don't you miss him, even just a little?" I asked

"Naw," she said. "The house is a lot quieter without him all the time getting mad and yelling. I don't miss him throwing his plate against the wall when Mama burns the meat, and I sure don't miss staying out of his way when he's drunk."

It seemed to me that her Mama never quite got over her Daddy's leaving. She got more disheveled looking, and sometimes she didn't cook or clean up the house for days.

"She took up where Daddy left off. With the drinking, I mean," Cate said. "But I don't mind. When she drinks, she just disappears and lets me fend for myself. As long as there's no fussing and fighting, she can drink for all I care."

As we got older, we didn't play dolls any more. Cate still told me movies, but she didn't get to see as many as she used to. Her family couldn't afford it. Sometimes she'd sneak in and watch them anyway, but she couldn't do that every single week. Instead, we swapped clothes and tried on lipstick that Cate stole from her

Mama's dressing table. We giggled and gossiped and pretended we were grown-up ladies. I had to scrub my face so hard afterward I thought my skin would wash right down the drain so Momma wouldn't see.

I was content to roam around the woods, making up stories and listening to Cate's movies, but Cate was cut from different cloth. She liked excitement, and for her that usually involved doing things she'd been warned not to.

"Let's go skinny-dipping in the river," she'd say. Or "Let's go get a pastry." Getting a pastry doesn't sound naughty, but when neither of us had any money, this involved her slipping two gooey sweet rolls into her coat pockets while I distracted the bakery clerk with respectful conversation about the weather or Mrs. Platt's gout, or some such thing. I felt awfully guilty about it because the clerk went to our church, but I never could resist Cate's half-scornful nagging.

"You're such a stick-in-the-mud," she'd say. "You need to have some fun. Take a risk."

That's what she said one evening when she wanted me to sneak out of the house after Momma went to bed.

"I can't do that, Cate," I said. "Even if Momma doesn't find out, Danny will. He'll tell on me. You know how he is."

Danny hadn't changed much as he got older. He was still fragile and sickly. He hadn't fleshed out, either, so he was still skinny. His hair stuck straight up off his head in spots and his wrists and elbows rolled around under his pale skin like empty thread spools. Momma'd stopped trying to get him to play sports, fearful he'd get snapped in half like a dry twig. Instead of scouts and baseball and 4-H, he devoted himself to school, and got straight A's.

"He'll be the first in our family to be college-educated," Momma said.

He was still a tattletale, too. There wasn't a chance on earth I could creep out of our room or, as Cate suggested, climb out the window, without waking Danny up and sending him pounding down the stairs to tell Momma, and so I told Cate.

"Fine," she said. "Be that way. You're going to die without ever having any fun at all, Miss Goody Two-Shoes."

I didn't see anything wrong with being good. It made life more peaceful to do what was expected of me. Besides, I got knots in the pit of my stomach when pursuing one of Cate's wild fancies. Getting knots in your stomach wasn't my idea of fun. I always expected a tap on the shoulder from some disapproving adult saying "What do you think you're doing, young lady?" Cate wasn't as fond of peace as I was. She thought it was boring.

"Why can't we go out during the day?"

"Because we just can't," she said.

"Well, where are you going, anyway?"

"I'm going to meet someone, if you really want to know."

"Meet who?"

"Someone. Oh, don't look at me like that. I don't have a boyfriend, if that's what you're thinking."

"Then who is it?"

"None of your business. If you want to know, you have to come."

"I can't."

"Then I guess you aren't going to know," she said, tossing back her heavy, blond hair.

"Cate, I wish you wouldn't."

"Oh, you're such a worry-wart. Jim's nice. We just drink a little, and he's teaching me to dance."

"Dance?"

"Yes, Sairy, dance. It's not like having sex in the middle of the street, you know. You don't have to give me that look."

"What look? I'm not looking at you."

"Yes you are. You don't even have to say anything." Cate screwed up her face in an eerily accurate imitation of Mrs. Moffat and said, "The Lord doesn't approve of dancing. You fear the Lord, don't you, Sairy?"

"Don't make fun of that, Cate. It's not funny."

Cate giggled. "Well, do you?"

"Of course I do. You should, too."

"I don't see why the Lord has a problem with dancing," she said.

"Because He just does. Because it's worldly. It leads to sin."

"No it doesn't. I'm not doing anything terrible. I'm just trying to have fun."

"Well, who's Jim?"

"Just someone I know."

"How come I never met him? Does he go to our school?"

"No, stupid. He's way too old for that. He doesn't go to any school."

"Cate, you shouldn't be going around with old men."

"He's not old, silly. He's 20."

To my 13-year old mind, 20 was as old as Momma. "That's really old," I said.

"No, it's not. Anyway, you better not say anything about this to your Momma. I swear, you're as bad as Danny. I'm sorry I asked you to come."

"I won't tell Momma," I promised. But I felt guilty about it. Who knows what kind of trouble Cate could get into drinking and dancing, and with an old man to boot? I wished Cate would settle down and be content with the milder type of fun we'd enjoyed as children.

She came back from these escapades, which got more frequent as our eighth-grade year progressed, with her eyes heavy from lack of sleep and an inner excitement that made her restless. Sometimes, she was sick and had to stay home from school.

I guess even then Cate was changing into a different kind of person. I had trouble keeping up. I wanted her to come to her senses and go back to being the old Cate. I spent more time thinking about how things should be than I did realizing how they actually were.

***

I guess things were hard for Cate's Mama after her Daddy left. She worked as a waitress and a clerk at the grocery store, but she kept losing her job.

"She goes on a drunk," Cate said, "and doesn't go in to work."

Cate's family moved out of their house, and they bounced from one place to another looking for something cheaper. Finally, when we got to High School, they moved back to her Mama's mother's house in Washington. I guess her Mama got tired of trying to make enough money to feed them all.

When Cate told me they were going, I couldn't stop crying. "How'm I going to do without you?" I wailed.

"You'll do okay," she said. "You've got your Momma and Danny."

"They're not you," I said. "I won't have anyone to talk to at school. Nobody cares anything about me except you."

"Well, you'll just have to make some more friends."

"I can't! I can't! Before I met you, everybody made fun of me. You're the only person that ever even tried to like me. Why do you have to go? Can't you stay here with us?"

"Oh, Sairy, don't cry. I'll miss you, too." She hugged and kissed me, and for a minute, the old Cate was back. But then, she let me go and fished a tiny mirror out of her purse and started checking to see whether her hair was messed up.

"You still have your headband, don't you?" I asked. Cate had stopped wearing it after her Daddy left.

"I still have it somewhere," she said. "But headbands are for babies."

"Well, don't lose it," I said. "You never know when you might need it."

"Okay," she said, putting her mirror back in her purse. "Say, Sairy. Since I'm leaving town and all, why don't we sneak out together one last time before I go?"

"I never snuck out before."

"Well, let's do it once, then."

"I can't."

Cate sighed. "Still the same, old Sairy."

"I'll never change," I said. "You'll always be my best friend."

She looked at me then, as if searching my face for something she didn't quite believe was there. "Will you?" she said.

"Forever," I promised.

***

I asked Momma the same question I'd asked Cate: couldn't Cate come and live with us? But Momma said "No. Her place is with her family. Besides, her Mama needs her to help look after the house. You can write to each other."

I wrote to Cate faithfully, telling her all the details I'd've shared if she was there.

"Danny got straight A's again," I'd write, "and Momma says he'll grow up to be a doctor or a lawyer. He says he wants to be an accountant, though."

"When I got up this morning, the chicken water was frozen solid, right to the bottom of the bowl. I guess winter's coming early."

"Mr. Cahill gave us some venison sausage. He shot two deer this year. I don't like venison much, but Momma says to count our blessings."

Cate responded with notes scrawled in large writing on postcards with pictures of Scenic Washington, or, one time, a giant potato on wheels stuck in the middle of the highway. "Famous Idaho Potatoes," it said. Her notes were brief and told me little about what she was doing. They got more and more sporadic, and finally dried up altogether. At last, my letters started coming back marked "Addressee Unknown."

So, in the middle of my first year at High School, I lost my only friend. Without Cate, I was rudderless. I had time to fill and nobody to spend it with. I missed the gossip and giggling, and even the arguments when Cate would insist on doing something I knew we shouldn't. I'd hidden my shyness behind Cate so long I didn't even know if I had a personality separate from hers. I moped around for months, couldn't figure out what to do with myself. Until I met Virgil.

## Chapter 6

# ᪥ Virgil ᪥

Virgil was a strong, quiet boy, the son of a logger and grandson of a logger. He moved up from Athol the same year Cate left, and I noticed him right away. He had eyes the color of granite and glistening brown hair that fell across one eye like a hunk of liver.

Like me, he didn't say much. Unlike me, he hung around with the popular boys, the ones that played football and were always whooping and shoving each other in the hall. He stood out from them because of his serious ways; it made him seem older than the others. His voice was low and gentle. I never heard him tease anyone or say anything mean.

He did right well in school, too, not a brain but well up in his classes. Somehow, he managed to get along with everyone, staying on good terms with kids in every clique without ever joining one. Sometimes, in his quiet way, he'd step between the jocks and some younger kid they were teasing, usually a hick like me, and he managed to do it without bringing their wrath down on his head.

"That's enough," he would say, and even the captain of the football team would listen to him.

Almost from the first day I saw him, I started taking him home in my dreams. When I cooked for Momma and Danny, I imagined I was cooking for Virgil. When I dressed for school in the morning, I tried to guess what his favorite color was and wore it. Before we'd ever spoken, he'd told me he loved me a hundred times, that I was the most beautiful girl he'd ever seen, that he'd been wanting to meet me ever since he'd first laid eyes on me. Just watching him walking through the hall or sitting kitty-corner from me in the lunchroom made my heart gallop like a runaway horse.

He was two years ahead of me, and for a while, those two years seemed an impassible gulf. He'd stand slightly apart, with his hands in his pockets and a tiny smile on his face, while his friends scuffled and traded insults in pretended hostility. He was on the football team and the basketball team. He wasn't a star, but good enough to make the varsity team as a second-stringer. I went to every game and waited for the coach to put him in so I could imagine him scoring a miraculous, game-saving touchdown and being carried from the field on the shoulders of his ecstatic teammates. I'd stand on the sidelines watching, not cheering, and his eyes would meet mine over the heads of the crowd.

"Who is that girl that's so different from the rest?" he would wonder. Then, after he showered, he'd come out of the locker room looking for me. He might even say to his friends "Did you see the girl that wasn't cheering? Who is she?" By that time, though, I'd have gone home, so he'd spend the whole rest of the weekend thinking about me. At school the next Monday, he'd search for me, maybe catch sight of me in the lunchroom and come over to sit at my table. "I noticed you last Friday," he'd say, "and I couldn't get you off my mind all weekend. Would you go steady with me?"

Of course, none of this happened. When he played, I cheered my head off. Sometimes, when the crowd was really loud and nobody could hear me, I'd yell out his name. Everyone else would be cheering for the quarterback, but I'd be yelling for Virgil. He never scored the winning goal. Our eyes never met. He never came over to me in the lunchroom. I sat alone, day after day, in the remotest corner of the room, picking at my homemade sandwich and dreaming about him.

Once, when I was rushing through the hall late for class, with my eyes fixed on the floor, I ran right, smack into him by accident.

"Oh! Excuse me," I said, my face burning red. "I didn't see you there."

"I guess not," he said. "What're you looking for on the floor? Did you drop something?"

"No," I said, backing away as quick as I could. "I was just trying to get to class on time."

One of his friends was standing with him. "Are all hicks as blind as you?" he snickered.

At that moment, I backed right into the wall, and banged my head on the handle of someone's locker.

"Ow," I said, putting my hand up to the back of my head. At this, Virgil's friend laughed outright. I turned from both of them and ran back up the hall toward the class I'd just left. I knew I'd be late to my next class, but I didn't care. I just wanted to get as far away from Virgil as I could.

Later, I remembered the way he'd spoken to me, not sneering like his friend, but matter-of-factly, like he just wanted to know what I was doing staring at the floor instead of watching where I was walking. I wished I could've come up with something clever to say, something that would've caught his attention. But even after the fact, with plenty of time to think about it, I couldn't. I just wasn't the clever type. I wasn't the pretty type, or the smart type, either, so that left me with no hope at all of making Virgil notice me.

I took my dreams to the loom...I had nowhere else to go with them. I couldn't tell anyone how desperately I loved him; I was embarrassed. For the first time in months, I was almost glad Cate was gone. She would've seen it right away, and demanded that I share my feelings with her. But the very thought of talking about it made me feel sick. I felt like my skin had been flayed off and exposed every nerve ending in my body to the rough touch of humiliation.

I spent most of my spare hours weaving, and Virgil was on my mind every minute. I dreamed that I was beautiful and fascinating, and boys were fighting each other over me, and Virgil won every fight. I dreamed about heroic rescues where evil men came to the school and threatened Virgil, and I hid him and refused to tell where he was, even under torture. I dreamed that he saved me from drowning in a flood after I'd plunged in to save someone's child. Any dramatic way a person could fall in love with another person, I dreamed about that happening between Virgil and me.

Every dream found its way into my weaving. The piece was chaotic with colors. They tangled around each other in a rich cacophony of glowing threads. From a distance, it looked gray, but up close, intricate patterns revealed themselves, subtle patterns that enticed your eyes deep into the story it told. I think it was the underlying feeling, not the details of the stories, that permeated it.

When I finished several narrow strips, I sewed them together and made curtains for the window in Danny's and my room. Every morning, the sun came through the window and lit those curtains with heavenly fire. It lifted my heart just to see the light play over them. When I looked at them, love didn't seem impossible like it did in real life, just delayed until the moment was perfect.

Virgil loved those curtains, too, although I never told him the dreams that were woven into them. After we married and got our own place, I hung them at our bedroom window to watch over us like a benevolent angel. I don't have them any more. I buried them with Virgil.

***

Lord knows whether we ever would have met if it wasn't for Danny. One hot day, during that summer after I first saw Virgil, Momma and Danny and I went to our favorite swimming hole on the Yaak River in Montana. It was a deep, clear hole, and on the far side, the river washed up against a huge slab of granite that climbed vertically out of the water like a retaining wall holding back the steep river bank. We kids used to climb up to ledges that seamed the rock face and jump off them into the river, the timid ones five feet up and the bravest ones all the way to the top, maybe 30 feet up. Danny and I stayed down on the lower ledges. Momma didn't want me going too high, she didn't feel it was ladylike, and Danny wouldn't climb to the top because heights made him dizzy.

That day, Danny and I swam across to the rocks and took turns with the other kids, climbing up and jumping off. We jumped, then floated downstream in the current, paddling gently until we washed up near the bank, then made our way through the shallows back up to where we could swim across and do it again.

There was a deep hole below the diving rocks, and there, the current slowed, but beyond the deep spot, the river became shallow and flowed swiftly over a series of rapids. We always made the far bank upstream from the rapids, as we didn't want to get swept around the bend and out of Momma's sight. Because he was younger and I was supposed to keep an eye on him, I made Danny dive first, and then I went after him. I told him to wait for me in the water, and we'd swim to the bank together.

We'd dove four or five times already that day, and I was getting a little bored with it. So, that last time, after Danny dove, I dawdled on the ledge for several minutes, generating some excitement by pretending I was getting ready to make a spectacular dive into the ocean from a hundred-foot rock, and posing on the brink for dramatic effect. I stayed there dreaming so long that the kids behind me in line started hollering at me to stop fooling around and jump already, and suddenly, I heard Danny calling my name.

"Sairy! Help me! My foot's stuck!"

"That kid. What a baby," I said to no one in particular, just showing off for the other children by acting all put upon.

Still, I stopped my fooling around and jumped into the water after Danny, a little peeved at him for messing up my fantasy and wondering what in the Sam Hill he was fussing about. When I reached the place where he was, right on the upper edge of the rapids, he was crying that his foot was jammed in between two rocks and he couldn't get it loose. "It hurts," he said. Sure enough, he'd got it twisted between and half under two big rocks in a spot where the current was so swift I could hardly keep from being torn loose and swept downstream. I held on to a rock with one hand and tried to pry his foot out with the other, but he kept crying that it was hurting him. Meanwhile, the current was trying to sweep him along, too, and was darn near wrenching his knee out of its socket because of the jammed foot.

"Momma!" I hollered, and waved toward the shore where Momma was sitting under a tree knitting. "Momma! Danny's foot is stuck! His knee is getting broken!"

Momma was pretty far off. The noise of the water rushing through the rapids was too loud for her to hear. She didn't even look up from her knitting.

I gave up trying to get his foot loose, and instead tried to hold the current off him so's his knee wouldn't get messed up. I struggled upstream a foot or two, wedged myself against a rock, and then pulled him up to my downstream side. Both my arms were now taken up with holding Danny. "Try to get your foot undone," I ordered.

"I can't, I can't, Sairy," he said, now sobbing. "I'm scared. How're we gonna get out of here?"

"Stop crying," I said, but he just cried harder.

"Hey, kid," said a voice. "Don't cry. You'll be okay."

I looked up to find Virgil's gray eyes inches away from my face. He'd arrived at the swimming hole with a large group of boys from the school. He told me later he'd come climbing down the hill from the road with his friends and seen Danny crying. The other boys stood on the river bank hooting crybaby, but Virgil felt sorry for him and swam out to help. Between the two of us, we worked Danny's foot out from under the rocks and helped him over to the bank. We avoided the boys by walking upriver a ways while still in the shallows close to the bank, and half-carried him over the boulders to where Momma was sitting.

"Why Danny, what on earth happened to you?" Momma said.

"He got his foot stuck under a rock," I said. "The current was pulling him so fast we couldn't get it undone, and it wrenched his knee."

"Oh honey," said Momma. "You sit down right here and let me wrap it up."

"Virgil helped me get him loose, Momma," I said, and then blushed because I'd said Virgil's name out loud to another person for the first time.

"Virgil," Momma said, "I surely thank you. Are you one of Sairy's friends from school?" Well, now I was ready to sink into the ground. Of course Virgil didn't even know I was alive.

"That's right," said Virgil. He gave me a glance out of the corner of his eye and I read a twinkle there. If I could've melted into a puddle of butterscotch, I surely would've. Being so close to him made me feel faint. "My name's Virgil Talbert, ma'am."

"Mrs. Ida Perdy," she said, shaking his hand from where she knelt in front of Danny. "I'm glad to know you, Virgil. I guess Sairy must have been mighty glad to have your help."

"Yes," I mumbled.

"It was my pleasure, ma'am. I'd better get on back to my friends now." Then he turned to me and said "I'll see you at school, Sairy Perdy."

When Momma was finished fussing over Danny, tying up his knee with a couple of napkins from our food basket, she declared it was time to go. Danny always was a fragile boy, scaring easily and not getting over it quick, and now he was pale and still a little teary. We had to half-carry him up the steep, rocky path to the road. While we did, Momma interrogated me about Virgil.

"I never heard you mention your friend Virgil before. Who is he?"

"He's not exactly a friend, Momma. He's an older boy. He was new last year."

"Older? How much older?"

"He's going to be a Senior this year."

"Does he go to church?"

"I don't know, Momma. I expect so. I don't know him all that well. But you can see how nice he is. All the other boys just stood on the bank and called Danny a crybaby. Virgil was the only one that helped."

"Well, you be careful of him, Sairy. I don't want you dating any wild boys. You need to find yourself a good, churchgoing boy." Momma had strict standards. She wasn't about to condone future misbehavior just because someone helped Danny get untangled from the river.

"Aw, Momma," I said. "He's never asked me on a date."

"Well, that's good," she said. "You're too young for all that mess. You get yourself through school before you start thinking about boys."

I hoped she was wrong. I hoped I wasn't too young for Virgil. I could already see myself standing beside him in a white dress with a bouquet of daisies in my hands. I floated up to the road on a pink cloud. I kept seeing his granite eyes sliding sideways to twinkle at me and hearing his voice say "I'll see you at school, Sairy."

Of course, school didn't start for weeks. By then, I knew, he could've forgotten all about me. Never before had I longed for the drudgery of school, but now I fretted as the remaining days of vacation crawled past like dragging an 80 pound bag of chicken feed through deep snow.

When the first day of school finally came, I put on my prettiest dress and tied a ribbon in my hair. I stumbled when I got off the bus; my knees were weak with anticipation. I didn't see Virgil all day, and in fact, I didn't see him for a whole week. I found out later he'd been with his father's sister in Moses Lake. That week was agony. I figured he'd moved away and I'd never see him again.

By the time he came back to school, I'd given up hope of ever seeing him again. The day I did, I was wearing a ratty old hand-me-down dress from the thrift store, faded, with a bright strip around the hem where Momma'd had to let it down. I was sitting down by myself in the lunch room, just getting ready to open up my paper sack, when suddenly he appeared standing across the table.

"Hi, Sairy," he said. My heart started pounding, and my face felt like ants were crawling all over it.

"Hi," I said.

"How's your little brother?"

"Oh, he's just fine. His knee hurt for a while, but he's back to his usual shenanigans now, as Momma says."

"He get in trouble a lot?"

"No, I'm the one that gets in trouble."

"You get in trouble? That's hard to believe," he said.

"Momma says I don't act ladylike," I explained, and then wished I could cut out my tongue. Why was I telling him this? He just crinkled up his eyes in a little smile.

"You look like a lady to me," he said. "You mind if I sit here?" He sat down on the bench across from me and opened up his own sack. I was so nervous I could barely swallow, but at the same time, my heart was singing for joy. We talked about….oh, I don't know what. Everything he said sounded momentous to me, but I don't remember any of it now. All I remember is the excitement and anxiety of being close to him. Every time I said something, I thought I sounded like a raving idiot, but Virgil told me later he thought I was cute and funny and a little bit shy.

Virgil was a careful, deliberate boy. It took a long time for him to get around to asking me out. He started eating lunch with me most days, and then, he began walking with me between classes. It was months before he asked me to go anywhere with him and then it was to a church picnic with his family. All his foot-dragging gave Momma a chance to be reconciled to the idea of me dating, and the church picnic was just the sort of outing she approved of.

I drifted through those months in a happy dream. The more I knew of Virgil, the better I loved him. Why he chose me, instead of all the girls in school that were smarter, prettier, or more personable, I never knew. We just seemed to flow together like two streams joining forces to become a river, each making the other fuller and stronger. I understood why he did that for me; I just didn't understand how I could do it for him. I asked him about it a few times after we married, but Virgil was never a big explainer. He just patted me and said, "I fell in love. That's all there was to it."

Early in my junior year, he asked me to marry him. After I got out of school and turned 18, of course. I was ready to marry him right then. What use was school for a married woman, anyway? But both Momma and Virgil were dead set against it. Virgil said he didn't need an ignorant wife, and Momma said I was too young; I had plenty of time to clean house and make babies *after* I turned 18.

Momma viewed Virgil with initial suspicion that only gradually dissipated into acceptance. She didn't start taking us seriously until after she'd met his family. She seemed to set a great store on how a person was raised. When it turned out Virgil's Ma and Pa were plain, Christian folk like us, only going to the Baptist church instead of the Nazarene, Momma said "Handsome is as handsome does. If he does right by you, I'll love him just fine," and I knew she wouldn't fuss over us getting married.

Virgil took it all in stride, the suspicion and the acceptance. He seemed to expect Momma to act just the way she did. He was polite and formal with her, always calling her "ma'am" and "Mrs. Perdy", and he didn't hesitate to help out with bucking up firewood or digging the garden. He was working, of course, as soon as he got out of school, but when he had a day off, he'd come up to Momma's and take on the more strenuous chores. I know Momma was grateful for that, although she never said so. She had a hard time being the man of the family as well as the woman.

# Chapter 7

# ❦ Married Life ❧

I had my wedding the day after graduation. It wasn't like a wedding you'd have nowadays. We had no money for bands and fancy dresses and catered dinners. Momma and I made the dress out of off-white satin she found in the lining of an evening dress at the thrift store in Spokane. We had to add material, so there was plain white mixed in with the satin, and yards of lace trim that Momma tatted out of fine cotton thread. We bought tulle and made a short veil, and the morning of the wedding, Momma gathered a bunch of daisies and gladioli from her flower garden. Virgil and I stood up in front of the preacher in the cramped, dark church and he joined us together before God and man until death us do part.

Even though death has parted us now, I still feel married to my Virgil. Our ties have lasted beyond the grave, despite the wedding vows that said death would end them. Virgil, Virgil. I still hear your deep voice steadying me, saying "Now, Sairy" when my mind is fluttering around like a butterfly and I can't figure out what to do. I still see your granite eyes sparkling at me across the breakfast table as you sniff the pancakes steaming from the griddle and say "buckwheat – my favorite." I still smell you on an early morning before I rise from my bed. The scent of the woods clinging to your hair and the comforting smell of man's sweat from a hard day's work linger in the bed these many years later.

Of course that can't be. These sheets've been washed a hundred times since then. But I drew you into my heart and you settled there like a stone in a hole...the stone's gone, but the hole remains. My heart must be a moonscape, where there's no wind or rain to erase the footprints a man makes walking across the ground.

How glad I am that Virgil never knew what I did. That way, my memories of him can be clean and wholesome, as our relationship was, as *he* was.

\*\*\*

After the wedding, we moved into a little apartment over a store on Main Street. We lived there for two years while Virgil built a cabin for us on Momma's land. The apartment was cramped and dark and smelled of bacon grease and cigarette smoke. Virgil hated that cigarette smell. Most of the men at the mill smoked, but Virgil would never allow it in our house.

Of course, he was gone for long hours each day, leaving me alone in the apartment. I spent my time scrubbing walls and beating carpets and washing windows until I'd gone over every inch of that apartment with soap and brush. But despite all my labor, I couldn't make the place feel clean. It was like an old, stained diaper that, wash as you will, never looks like new again. The cigarette smoke lingered, and a faint odor of mildew. The sunlight fell into the windows through a deep crack between two brick buildings. It lost so much of its life on the way down that it was never quite able to penetrate the gloom that pervaded the rooms like a constant fog, and I had the lights on most of the time, even in broad daylight.

The weekends were like getting a furlough from prison. Virgil and I would go up to Momma's. Us two women would sit on the porch and watch the cabin take shape, sipping tea or lemonade and talking about things married women talk about – the difficulty of organizing housework, the price of groceries and the little frustrations of living with a man. I'd help Momma with the canning. Sweating over the stove, which used to seem such a burden, was now a blessing compared with being cooped up in that dingy apartment.

Momma would've been glad to have me up during the week, but I didn't suggest it, nor speak a word of complaint about living in town. The apartment was the place my husband provided for us. I would've lived in a garbage can to be with Virgil, if I'd had to. I never told either of them how I missed the cool, tangle of the birch woods with the spring bubbling out of its secret heart, or the woodpeckers drumming on rotten trees in the morning, or the dry rasp of cicadas on hot summer nights.

In the country, being poor was nothing. The beauty of land and sky swallowed it up like an ocean swallowing a drop of ink, paying back in splendor what you couldn't buy with money. In town, the hand-me-down clothes and tattered shoes that seemed sensible when kneeling in the dirt or mucking out the chicken coop looked cheap and pathetic.

In town, I felt conspicuous, which was like school all over again. I like to blend into the background. I don't want folks noticing me. When I'm doing something noticeable, like singing in church, why, I just pretend it's someone else doing it. I, the real Sairy, am hidden away, secret. The person they notice is just a shell. In town, I felt like I couldn't escape being noticed. I was too different from everyone else. It was as if I had a sign around my neck saying "Sairy the hick."

We moved into our cabin right before the first snow. It didn't take long; we had few belongings. Virgil borrowed a truck from someone at work and piled our things in the back. They got wet in the rain, and I lit a fire first thing and hung our clothes and bedding up to dry on lines strung all over the house. Then I wiped the water off everything else and put it out on the open shelves Virgil built out of scrap lumber he got from the mill.

His parents had given us a late wedding gift: a brand new wood cook stove built by an Amish man in Pennsylvania. Not knowing it was coming, Virgil'd bought an old stove from someone south of town whose parents had left it rusting in the barn when they put in gas. He'd buffed the rust off of it and blacked it up so it'd look nice in the house. When we got the new one, he put the old one out on the porch to use during the summer months for canning and such. I felt like royalty having two stoves, and being able to escape the stifling heat when it was too nice to have a fire indoors.

It was glorious to be back in the country, away from sterile, paved streets and cracked brick buildings. Our cabin was in the field, looking out to the mountains in the south and west, and backed up against the draw so the birch leaned over the porch, casting cool shade in summer and rattling dry fingers over the roof when the wind blew.

I still live there. Momma's old house under the pine trees is still there, too, but decrepit with age. No one's lived there for, oh, these twenty years. The fire hasn't been lit and the walls inside are musty with ancient damp. I suppose the roof'll give out one of these days, and the whole thing'll subside back into the land like a decaying corpse. Dust to dust, as the Bible says. I can see the house from the porch of my cabin. Sometimes I think I catch a glimpse of smoke rising from the chimney, just as it used to do on crisp, fall mornings when Momma was baking bread.

We lived in separate houses, but we were knit together in one working unit. Now that we were married, Momma deferred to Virgil as the head of the family. If he wanted to plant somewhere, we planted. If he wanted to cut timber, we cut it. If he wanted to put up a fence, we put it up.

Virgil gradually managed the land into a new order. We put sheep and goats in the front pasture, a cow in the back, put a hog pen next to the chicken yard, which we expanded along with the garden. Momma's flowers, which used to spread higgledy-piggledy all over the property, were contained in neat boxes in front of her house...Virgil said we couldn't waste good land on fal-lals.

I fed stock, canned vegetables, dried fruit, washed eggs and made cheese out of the goats' milk and butter from the cows'. Those were busy times, but I was young and strong and in love. I would've walked to Hell and back for Virgil. I wanted nothing more than to make a good life for our family. Being married to him was even better than my dreams.

We didn't talk a lot. Virgil was never chatty. But he stood under my life like a solid, stone foundation that nothing could shake. Before I knew Virgil, I used to flit around like a dragonfly, thinking aimless thoughts and spending most of my time daydreaming as I wandered from one half-finished task to another. After I married him, I steadied down. My mind was organized around the work I had to accomplish every day for *his* sake. We were one person, just as the Bible says, only I wanted to work for him more than for myself. If my stomach growled, I might put off fixing lunch in favor of picking lupine in the field, but if Virgil was hungry, I could think of nothing else until he was fed. Even the flesh on his bones was precious to me.

Virgil matched my devotion with his own. He worked at the mill and then came home and worked on the property. When we fell into bed at night, exhausted from the day's work, he'd put his arm under my head and say, "Another day gone, Sairy. A good day."

Sunday was the only day we didn't work. It pleased Momma, and it pleased me too, that Virgil reverenced the Sabbath just as we thought proper. I've met so many wives who believe differently from their husbands. That wasn't so for us. We fit together like a two puzzle pieces...soul mates I believe they call it now.

I don't know about soul mates. It seems to me folks have to play the hand the Lord deals 'em and conform to the spouse they have, not go looking for a better one. If they don't like the one they marry, seems it's their own fault most times. But I was lucky in Virgil. He could've turned out to be a drinker or a lazy man. I'd've fallen in love with him just the same, and I'd've had to love him through the years. Just God's grace he was such a man as he was, and living with him was as easy as living in my own head.

***

After several years, Virgil bought a tractor. When he got that, he quit the mill and started farming in earnest, adding a few beef cattle and growing hay for the stock. He spent long days in the fields, mending fence, digging a well, bringing in the hay. I brought his lunch out to him and we'd sit in the shade with our backs to a tree and eat together. Oh, those were halcyon days!

The only thing that wasn't going so well was our family...we didn't have one.

"Where are my grandchildren," Momma wanted to know.

"I don't know, Momma," I'd say. "It's not like we aren't trying."

"D'you think there's something wrong with me?" I'd ask Virgil. "Maybe I should go to the doctor."

"What's the point?" he'd say. "If we have children, we have them. If we don't, we don't. It's the Lord's will."

"But honey. You deserve a family. And I want one." Secretly, I think I feared he might leave me if we had no children. A man wants children to carry on his name. And I longed for a child. How I loved the idea of blending Virgil's best with mine: his quiet confidence and my dreaminess, his granite eyes and my sturdy strength.

In the early years, I was convinced the children would come eventually. You sow seed, and some of it must sprout. It wasn't until later I realized they wouldn't, and tried to take matters into my own hands.

# Chapter 8

# ❦ Cate and Gilly ❧

It would've been six or seven years after we moved back to Momma's that we heard from Cate. I had no idea where she'd gone. After that last letter was returned "Addressee Unknown", I'd heard nothing from her. I'd have liked to invite her to my wedding. In fact, there were many things I'd have liked to share with Cate: what it was like to be a married woman, the loneliness of living in town, the joy of returning to the country...

But she'd dropped out of my life like a dead person, and over the years, I'd come to think of her like that. She was part of my childhood, maybe the best part, but long over. Virgil had replaced her at the heart of my life. So I was shocked when Momma, who'd gotten a phone at last, came running over to tell me she'd called.

"Sairy, honey, I just got a long distance call from the city."

I didn't even think to ask which city. "Who was it?" I said instead.

"It was your little friend, Cate."

"Cate? Our Cate called you? Why, I haven't heard from her in years. I didn't even think she remembered us."

"Yes, she remembers us. In fact, she wants to come home. She said she's moving back this way. I told her we'd be happy to put her up."

"Cate's moving back here?"

"Yes, child. She's coming right away."

Cate had moved away from her grandparents' house right after graduating from high school. She'd gone off to secretarial college and gotten a job typing letters and taking dictation and such for a businessman in a big office. She didn't tell Momma

much about what was going on there, just that things hadn't
worked out so good and she needed to get away and start over
again somewhere else.

Momma would've taken anyone in. She felt it was her
Christian duty to be hospitable. But in Cate's case, it was more
than a duty. Momma'd come to love Cate like her own daughter,
and she saw this as a homecoming.

But this Cate who came to live with Momma was a new
Cate. We had to get acquainted all over again. She arrived at
Momma's house with one giant suitcase and a little train case,
which she carried up to the old room where Danny and I used to
sleep, picking her way daintily through the house like she was
afraid the primitive condition of it would rub off on her. After
dumping her case in the middle of the bed, she minced back down
to the kitchen table and perched on the edge of a chair, waiting for
Momma to finish making tea and looking around the house like
she didn't remember it. She wore city clothes, too tight and
expensive for farm work, and high-heeled shoes, and makeup.
Under all the powder and rouge, her face looked strained and
unhappy. She had a gloss of discontentment all over her like a
hard shell.

"Lord, I'd forgotten you-all had a privy," she said, making
a face like maybe she thought we'd added a bathroom on just for
her. "When are you going to catch up with the real world?"

"A privy's good enough for us, young lady," Momma said.
"There's no one to carry your slops in this house. Everyone does
for herself around here." Momma might love Cate, but to her, love
included an obligation to watch over your character, make sure
you weren't falling into self-indulgence and other sinful ways.

"Virgil says maybe we'll put in running water next year," I
added eagerly. "Then you can come use our bathroom." I wanted
Cate to be happy here. I saw us re-establishing the sisterhood of

our youth. I didn't want her getting disgusted and moving back to the city.

"Oh…it doesn't matter," Cate said, picking restlessly at her fingernails. These were long and painted red to match her lipstick.

"Why don't you change out of your nice clothes and come sit down on the porch," Momma suggested. "We can have our tea out there."

"Change into what?" Cate said. "This's all I've got."

"Land sakes," said Momma. "What's in that big suitcase of yours? Sairy, why don't you go see if you can find something Cate can wear around the farm? Something that won't get ruined by all our dirt."

I ran home and grabbed the first thing I could find, one of my old house dresses, faded to gray and soft with age and wear. When I handed it to Cate, she eyed it with distaste. Next to her bottle green, wool skirt and white silk blouse it looked sorry indeed. "I don't know if this'll fit," she said.

"I've got others," I said. "I just grabbed the first thing that came to hand. You don't have to wear it. Don't you worry. We'll find something for you."

"Maybe later," she said.

"So," Momma said, lapsing comfortably into another chair, "you must've been up to some exciting things. Tell us about what it's like to live in the big city."

Cate bit her lip and looked like she might cry. "It's nothing much," she said. "I'd rather not talk about it."

Momma patted her hand. "Well, you're home now, dear," she said. "You can see we're eye deep in animals now. There'll be plenty to do helping Sairy out around the place. Land sakes, I hardly move any more except to bake and clean house. Sairy does most of the canning and gardening, and she and Virgil look after the animals."

Cate didn't look enthused. I imagined her teetering out to the chicken yard in her spike heels, picking her way around the cow pies, and giggled.

"What's so funny," she said, glaring at me.

"Nothing," I said. "I was just imagining you trying to slop hogs in those shoes."

"Well, I haven't been doing a lot of hog-slopping," she said.

Indeed, as the days went by, I wondered what she *had* been doing. She stayed in bed late, trailing downstairs hours after we'd all eaten breakfast to pick at her cold toast and coffee. She wouldn't light the stove. She wouldn't weed the garden. She wouldn't feed the animals or wash eggs. But she didn't appear refreshed by all that nothing-doing, either. Instead, her face was gray and strained, and she slept restlessly or not at all. Gone were her sparkling (and naughty) laughter and zest for the simple pleasures that had once filled our hours together.

Through her eyes, I saw our life as sordid, filled with hours of filthy, backbreaking work. Things that were quick and easy for other folks, with their appliances and gas and what-have-you, we did by hand. Washing and bathing couldn't be done without hauling water, splitting wood and sweating over a hot stove. Instead of buying food at the store, all portioned out in a nice bag or box, we butchered, plucked, skinned and cleaned. Or we spent hours bent over the garden and more hours washing and canning. These things'd never bothered me before. The work had a slow rhythm to it, much like weaving, that made me feel peaceful inside. But Cate didn't seem to feel the rhythm or the peace...to her, it was just drudgery. She'd stand with her arms folded and her lips compressed and watch me scrub the floor or rinse the laundry.

"What's wrong?" I'd ask. "Why are you scowling?"

"Nothing," she'd say. "I'm not scowling." Then later, when I was done, she'd say "Don't you ever want something better than all this?"

"Why, no," I'd say. "What's wrong with it? I've got a good man and a good life."

"But it's so hard."

"Well, yes, I guess it's hard. But a body's got to do something, keep busy. Honey, I don't think I'd like working in an office. Wearing stockings and Sunday clothes all the time. Indoors all day. I lived in town when Virgil and I were first married, and I hated it. I felt like I couldn't stretch out like I needed to."

She wrinkled her nose. "But it's dirty here. And the animals stink."

"Those animals don't stink. We keep our animals clean and well-tended."

"Sairy, you're country through and through. But you can't expect me to like this. I wasn't raised for this. I'm used to something different."

"You used to like it up here. We had fun together. You liked the woods and the garden and the peace and quiet. I thought that's why you came back."

"Oh Sairy, I don't know why I came back. I thought maybe things would be better if I did, that maybe I could be happy again like I was back then."

"Why aren't you happy, Cate?" I asked.

"I don't know," she said.

Some nights, when Virgil and I were listening to the radio or getting ready for bed, we'd hear a car come up the driveway to Momma's house, then go back down a few minutes later. Cate, all dressed up in her fancy town clothes, would go out honky-tonking. At least, that's what Momma called it. I've never set foot in a bar in my whole life, so I don't know what goes on in there. But according to Momma, it's licentiousness and debauchery, a modern-day Babylon.

"Momma, something's wrong with Cate," I said.

"She's sick in her soul, Sairy," Momma said.

"Well, what can we do about it? We have to do something."

"Sometimes there's nothing to be done. Just love her as best you can, and pray the Lord will heal her."

So then I'd badger Virgil about it. "Virgil, Cate's not the way she used to be. She never stuck up her nose at me before."

"People change, Sairy."

"I haven't changed."

"Maybe you've changed more than you think."

"But I love it here. And Cate used to love it, too. This was the only place she was really happy. Why would she lose that?"

"I don't know."

We left Cate to herself. Momma tended to her, making her tea and toast, washing up after her, washing and pressing her fancy clothes with tender care. Despite what she'd said about everyone taking care of themselves, and despite how she'd brought me up, she didn't place any demands on Cate. She seemed to sense, as we all did, some brokenness inside her.

Things went on like this for several months, with Cate rattling around like a dried pea in a box, until she finally told me the root of her unhappiness: she'd sinned with a married man over in the city. That wasn't how she put it. What she said was that she'd "gotten involved" with her boss. It was, as Momma would've said, an old story. The man told her he didn't love his wife any more and she didn't love him. She was committing adultery on him, he said, which gave him latitude to be rid of her, and he was looking for a good woman to marry and settle down with. They were going to divorce; the wife wanted it as much as he did. Then he'd marry Cate and she could quit working and take care of his home. They'd have children together.

Of course, it turned out to be lies. He'd said the same thing to the girl before Cate and the girl before her. When Cate started pushing too hard, wanting to set a date for the wedding, wanting him to meet her Mama, wanting to stop sneaking around in sleazy motels, he told her the truth. He'd never divorce his wife, he said. She needed to grow up and realize she was what she was, just another home-wrecking whore like all the rest. If she hadn't been, she'd have never gone out to work in an office in the first place, would've stayed at home like a good girl and found herself a husband.

I was shocked. I never thought Cate would do something like that. "Cate, honey, you shouldn't have done that. You shouldn't have gone with a married man."

"It was his fault," Cate insisted. "He lied to me."

"But you knew he was married."

"He said he loved me. He said he would marry me."

"But honey, you don't want to marry a divorced man. And even if you did, he should've left his wife first, not carried on with both of you at the same time."

"I loved him, Sairy," she said. "I loved him so bad. I thought he would take care of me."

I tried to understand the kind of love that would cause someone to do something as horrendous as adultery. If Virgil had teased me to sin with him before marriage, I thought (which he never would have), I would have said 'no'. Momma taught me that a man would never respect a woman who gave in like that, no matter how hard he begged her, and it looked like she was right. I wasn't sure letting a woman go to work like a man was a good idea if it led to things like this, and I told Cate so.

"You don't understand, Sairy," she said. "You've always had your momma, and now you've got Virgil looking after you.

85

What would you have done if you were all alone? A person has to eat."

"You weren't alone," I said. "You had your mama."

"Not the way you think," she said. "Mama was getting so bad. Her parents kicked her out because they didn't like all her drinking. We moved from place to place running from one landlord and then another, sneaking out in the middle of the night so they wouldn't call the law on us. We finally moved in with Daddy's daddy, and he and Mama fought like cats and dogs every day. I couldn't wait to get out of there. Then my Grandpa gave me money for secretarial school, and told me 'You're on your own now. Don't come running to me for your bread and butter.'"

"Why didn't you come back here?" I said. "Me and Momma were here. We would've taken you in."

"I know," she said. Then she stared off at the mountains for several minutes, like making up her mind whether to say something. "I – I didn't want to live like you, Sairy," she finally said.

"What's wrong with the way I live?"

"It was fine when we were kids," she said. "The privy and no running water and the wood cook stove and all that. We always had fun. But when you grow up, it's different. You want a – a cleaner way of life."

"But we're not dirty," I protested. "We keep a clean house."

"I know, but it's…you're hicks."

There was that word again. I remembered Momma saying it was ignorant folks' way of calling us poor, and I told Cate that.

"Well, you *are* poor," Cate pointed out.

"Poor in money, maybe," I said. "But we've got all we need here."

"But you have to work so hard. I want the better things in life. I want a car and a nice house and nice clothes and all the modern conveniences. I don't want to haul buckets of water and split wood in order to cook."

This was reasonable. I could see her point. But didn't the good Lord deal each of us the hand He knew was best?

"The good Lord, the good Lord," Cate said impatiently. "Sairy, there're folks all over the world starving to death. What is the good Lord doing for them?"

Cate had me there. I didn't know what to say. So instead, I asked her "What are you going to do now?"

She shook her head. "I don't know," she said. "I can't stay here with you-all forever."

"Yes, you can," I said. "You can just stay here with us. I know you'll feel better after while, Cate. Just try," I coaxed her. "Just try and accept the way things are. I know you can do it if you keep trying."

"But I don't want to," she said. After that, she wouldn't talk about it any more. Whenever I tried to bring it up again, or offer to take her to church and introduce her to some young man there, she'd just shake her head.

*** 

It was a few months later that she came home from one of her nights out on the town with a whole new attitude. She usually slept in late, particularly after she'd been out. But this morning, she rose early and put on one of her older dresses, prim and neat where Momma had pressed the cuffs and collar, serviceable, but not tight and formal looking like so many of her things. She walked on over to our place when I was still setting breakfast on the table. I put out an extra plate and started shoveling eggs and pancakes and sausages on it.

"Don't give me that," she said. "I'm not eating all that greasy stuff." Virgil raised his eyebrows at her from over the pages of his Farmers Almanac. "It's all well and fine for *you*," she told him. "You're a big, hungry farm hand." It hurt my feelings a little the way Cate was always a bit snippy to Virgil. He was kind to her, and never criticized how she didn't do her share of the work or how me and Momma waited on her. I figured he deserved more consideration.

"I'll have some of that coffee," she announced, and I obligingly fetched her a cup. Unlike most mornings, when her blond hair was snarled and stiff with last night's hair spray, or limp and oily like a wet dishrag, today it glowed an ethereal gold and fell in gentle waves across her shoulders. Her blue eyes sparkled with enthusiasm. She sat silently sipping her coffee until Virgil gave me a kiss on the cheek and went out to feed the stock.

"It's good to see you up early," I said.

"Oh Sairy," she said, "Just wait'll I tell you what happened last night. I met someone."

"You met someone?" I said, not understanding.

"Yes, and he is perfect. Glorious. The man of my dreams."

"Oooh," I said. "You met a new boy. Well, who is he? Where'd you meet him?"

"Never mind that," she said. It didn't occur to me at the time, but later I figured she'd met him in some dance hall somewhere, and didn't want me criticizing. "His name is Gilly, and I'm in love with him."

"Not – not Gilly Faber," I said. Everybody in town knew the Fabers. Gilly Faber was born and reared here, and he was the wildest of the wild boys. His real name was Gilbert, but everyone called him Gilly. He'd been ahead of Virgil in school, so I didn't know him real well, but I'd come up with one of his brothers, Carson, that we called Sonny. Sonny was a bully and a troublemaker, and if rumor was right, he was a carbon copy of his older brother, Gilly.

When Gilly was eighteen, he'd been caught breaking into the gun shop downtown. Because his daddy was a manager at the mill, they didn't throw Gilly in jail; instead, they let him join the army. After the army let him go, he'd stayed in the city a while. Every so often we'd hear something about his exploits, how he'd gotten in a knife fight with someone's jealous husband. I hadn't heard he was back. Me and Virgil never ran in the same circles as Gilly.

"Cate, you can't fall in love with Gilly Faber. He's a wicked man. I've – I've heard terrible stories about his brawling and drinking."

"Oh, you and your churchy ways," she said. "Gilly's a *real* man. He's strong, and he doesn't care for what anyone says. Besides, he told me I'm the best-looking girl he's seen since he left the city." I could believe this. Cate was beautiful even as a child, slender and ethereal with golden hair and finical ways. And she had a fragile rapture about her that made you want to join in with what she was doing and protect her all at the same time. I feared Gilly would break her like a dry twig.

"But Cate," I faltered. "Gilly's wild, and he's mean."

"He's not mean to me," she said. "He treats me like a princess. That's what he calls me: 'princess.'"

Much as I didn't want Cate to be hurt, I hoped Gilly would decide she wasn't his cup of tea. "You just be careful of him," I said.

Cate had never been careful, and she paid no attention to my warning. Instead, she started going out to meet Gilly almost every night. One evening, he drove to our place to pick her up. I met him on the porch, curious to see what a wild boy looked like. He was big and beefy, and his ruddy hair was plastered to his head with something that looked like shoe polish. He wore jeans and boots and a cowboy shirt with red piping and roses embroidered on the yoke. His eyes were pale and small, and they surveyed me thoroughly and then looked away, bored, as if to say I wasn't much.

"Can I help you?" I asked.

"You Sairy?"

"Yes, I'm Mrs. Talbert."

"I'm here to get Cate," he said. "She's supposed to be ready."

"I'll call her. Won't you come in and have some coffee?"

"Nah. I'm looking for something a little harder than that." He stuffed his hands in his pockets and rocked back and forth on his feet, staring around at the house.

"This your place?"

"It's my husband's and mine, yes."

"Who's your husband?"

"Virgil Talbert."

"Oh yeah. He used to work for my Pa. What happened to him?"

"Nothing. He quit the mill to work on our place."

Gilly fished a toothpick out of his pocket and stuck it in his mouth. "Some place," he said, but it didn't sound like a compliment. "He build this?" He nodded toward the house.

"Yes."

"Uh huh. Well, tell Cate I'm here, okay?"

I left him on the porch, sucking his toothpick, and walked over to Momma's. I found Cate upstairs, fussing with her hair in front of the mirror.

"Gilly's here looking for you," I said.

"Okay," she said, and started smoothing her blouse over her figure, turning this way and that.

"Well, aren't you coming out?"

"Just let him wait a few," she said. "It keeps his interest if he thinks I don't care."

I walked back over to my house. Gilly had gotten tired of standing and deposited his bulk into a chair. He'd tipped the chair onto its back legs with its back against the wall and stretched his boots out straight.

"Where's she at?"

"She says she'll be down in a few minutes."

"She needs to get herself moving. I ain't got all night."

I sat in the chair beside him and primly folded my hands in my lap.

"Where do you-all go to church?" I asked.

"I ain't a churchgoing man," he said. "Ma goes to the Methodist."

"That's nice."

"So what do you-all do for fun out here?"

"Fun?"

"Yeah, you know. Fun. Your man make 'shine? You go dancing?"

"No. We don't drink."

"Uh huh."

"Where do you work, Mr. Faber?"

"You could say I'm between jobs. Sometimes I work for my Pa."

"Isn't that nice, you work as a family."

He made a snorting noise.

He kept tipping his chair back and letting it fall forward again, and I stared at my hands.

"Cate been out here with you-all long?"

"She and I grew up together," I said. "She's been back with us for several months now."

"Don't look like the kind of place she'd be living at."

"She's staying with us while she gets on her feet. She was living in the city before this."

"Yeah, I heard about that."

He rocked some more, and I stared some more.

"Where's your man?"

"Virgil went to town for feed. He'll be back shortly."

"That what he does in town? Buy feed?"

"Well, or whatever we need."

Gilly took a pack of cigarettes from his shirt pocket, fished one out and lit it. We sat without talking as he smoked it, then he threw the burning butt off the porch. Finally, I saw Cate picking her way along the path from Momma's house in her high heels. Even now, Gilly didn't straighten up in his chair.

"It's about dang time," he said.

"Sairy," Cate said, pretending to ignore him, "Would you look at the back of this skirt and make sure there isn't a thread hanging? I thought I saw something, but I was in too much of a hurry to take it off again." She turned around backwards so Gilly and I could get a good look at the back of her skirt. It was one of her nice, wool ones that was cut straight and fit close.

"I don't see anything," I said.

"Neither do I," said Gilly. Cate flashed him a look over her shoulder and tossed her hair back.

"Like you would know," she said.

"Are we going out, or we standing here all night looking at your...skirt?" Gilly said.

"Is that what you were looking at?" She turned around again and put her hands on her hips. "Are you going to just sit there like a boor? Or are you escorting me to the car?"

"Ess-korting you," he mocked. "Now get moving."

He dropped the chair's front legs on the floor and stood up, hauling up his pants and tucking in his shirt. As they walked to Gilly's pickup, he made a grab for her waist, but she batted his hand away, giggling.

Shortly after that evening, she reported that he was pressing her to have man-and-wife relations with him, but she'd learned her lesson with her boss over in the city and wouldn't give in until they were married. I couldn't figure out how to feel about it. While it was good she wasn't sinning with him, it was bad they were talking about getting married.

"Are you sure you'll be happy with him, Cate? He doesn't seem to treat you very nice."

"He's a man. He acts like a man."

"Virgil's a man, and he doesn't act like that."

"Sairy, I'm not talking about Virgil. You haven't been out in the world. Virgil's the only man you know. Most men aren't like Virgil."

"Yes. But he's the right kind of man, a good man. You could find a man like that, too."

"Gilly's the man I want."

And Gilly is the man she got.

It was a wedding I couldn't rejoice over, and a wedding the likes of which I never hope to see again. Me and Momma and Virgil were there, of course, but no one else from Cate's family came. Mostly it was men from the mill that came with Gilly's Pa, along with some ex-soldiers and other boys Gilly went around with, and their girlfriends. At least, I guess they called themselves girlfriends, though they were more intimate than I was used to, hanging off the men's arms, giggling into their necks and such like. I tried to make conversation with one of them, but she kept getting distracted by remarks from the other girls and ungentle-manly teasing from the men, so we didn't say much to each other. She did tell me she lived out of town, and that's all I know about any of them to this day.

The wedding was at the Methodist church, officiated by Gilly's Ma's pastor. The reception was held at the fairgrounds down by the courthouse. They couldn't have it at the church because they served alcohol, which the Methodists wouldn't allow any more than our church, and Gilly and his friends got rip-roaring drunk. I'd never seen a drunk man, besides Cate's daddy, and I can't say I felt too comfortable. The three of us sat in a corner and watched Gilly drag poor Cate around in a circle on the floor, almost flinging her into his Pa's lap when he lost his balance. They all laughed a lot, but there didn't seem to be much mirth in all of it. At the end, Gilly went off with his friends, who knows where, after bending Cate over backwards and kissing her in a way as shocking as it was lascivious. I agreed with Momma that it wasn't a seemly way to treat your wife in public.

We waited for hours at the reception as the crowd got thinner and thinner, but Gilly didn't return. Instead of going home with her husband, as was proper after a wedding, Cate had to come back to Momma's house with us. Then, very late at night, or maybe early the next morning, his truck came roaring up our driveway and we heard yelling and honking over by Momma's place. Virgil had to get up out of bed and make sure Momma was all right over there by herself with all those wild men. They were spilling out the back of the truck, tumbling out on the driveway and shooting in the air. I was fearful Virgil'd get hurt, but he handled it with quiet authority, bundling Cate out of the house and into the truck with her suitcase and her train case, and ordering the men to think shame on themselves and pipe down because decent folks were trying to sleep.

Momma didn't have as much to say about it as I expected. She just shook her head and told me that poor Cate had made her bed and now would have to lie in it. Virgil just hugged me tight and told me not to worry, that folks couldn't do much to change someone once their mind was made up.

We didn't see much of Cate after the wedding. She and Gilly moved south of town, and she didn't come visiting for a long time. I went to see her house, of course, and brought her some linen towels I'd woven. She and Gilly lived in an old house behind the school. It wasn't full of modern conveniences like Cate said she wanted.

"It's just temporary," she told me, "until Gilly can get some money together for something better."

I looked around at the warped, stained wooden floor and the gas stove crusty with burned-on food and prayed that Cate would find what she was looking for.

## Chapter 9

# ❧ The Baby ❧

With Cate gone again, Virgil became, once again, the center of my life. We were happy together. Oh, we fussed at each other now and again, just to keep things interesting. He'd get in tired, and I'd ask him to hang some curtains or some other of what he called "frilly work". He'd snap that he had *real* work to do, it was his job to put food on the table and couldn't I hang my own curtains. I'd slam the dishes around as I put dinner on the table, announcing that he wasn't the only one that worked hard and how would he like to get his own dinner and wash his own dirty underwear. Then he'd put his arm around my waist and call me his sweet Sairy, and promise he'd hang the curtains tomorrow, and I'd kiss his chin and tell him I was an old shrew and he was the best man the world ever knew.

Our marriage was perfect in every way, except we had no children. When my monthly time was due, I'd hold my breath and pray it wouldn't come, but it came anyhow. I think this was the beginning of my wickedness. I couldn't let it go. I yearned for a baby, dreamed about having a baby, envied the women I saw pushing their children in strollers or carrying them into the church. I volunteered to sit in the nursery and pretended all the children were mine.

"Just one, Jesus," I prayed. "Give me just one child." Then I'd ask Virgil, "Don't you want a baby?"

"Of course I do," he said.

"You're not going to leave me if we don't have a baby, are you?"

"I married you for better or worse," he said. "If God doesn't see fit to bless us with a child, so be it."

He might accept it, but I didn't. As time went on, I started to feel rebellious, resentful. Other women had two, three, even four. Why did I have none? It wasn't fair. I stopped praying, stopped even pretending to accept our childless state. I was desperate, and so I took matters into my own hands...I decided to weave a layette. In faith, I'd weave the layette, and then the baby would be born. I should've known you can't bargain with God.

Once I made up my mind to weave, I was obsessed by it. It would have to be the softest cotton there was, of course. I couldn't put a baby in rough clothes. Not even the warps could be stiff, so I strung the loom with fine, soft cotton thread, the kind Momma tatted lace out of. It tangled and broke easily, so it was slow work. The tedium didn't bother me. Patiently, I spent an hour sorting out the warps every time I unrolled the loom, careful not to break any as I picked through the knots. Tenderly, I threaded the weft through the sheds, patting it with a needle rather than beating it so I wouldn't fray the warps.

Slowly, the web took shape. I could smell the downy head of the baby as I wove, see its little arms gyrating as I bathed it, hear its inarticulate sucking noises in my ear as I toted it over one shoulder, going about my daily work. By the time the first piece was finished, I knew that baby's body, its scents and noises, as intimately as I knew Virgil's or my own. I ignored my monthly cycles, convinced I had already conceived. The baby, if a girl, would not be named Sairy, I decided. I'd name her Jonquil or Lupine or Rose...some name worthy of her miniature perfection. If a boy, it would be Virgil, of course, a sturdy name so he'd grow up like his daddy.

The baby was more real to me than my actual life. I neglected my work to spend hours at the loom. After dreaming and weaving all day, I'd throw down the loom just an hour before Virgil came in, race out to the wood shed, whack up some kindling, throw a few pork chops on the stove and swipe the broom hastily over the floor.

"What are you working at?" Momma asked, coming over day after day to find me sitting at the loom instead of doing my housework. "These windows are filthy. You can hardly see out them."

"I know, I'll get to it."

"That's what you said last week. Virgil didn't even have toast yesterday because you haven't made bread in days. There's a pile of laundry in your room almost as high as you. What's wrong with you, Sairy?"

"Nothing."

"Well, there must be something wrong. It isn't like you to neglect Virgil."

"Can't I borrow some bread from you, Momma? You baked yesterday."

"Of course you can have some of my bread. But why aren't you making your own?"

"I'm busy, Momma."

"Busy doing what?"

"Busy weaving."

Momma shook her head. "Nothing good will come of this."

"It will, Momma. You'll see."

To appease her, I set the weaving aside during the day, and only wove in the evenings. Some nights, though, I stayed awake long after Virgil had gone to bed.

I worked on the layette for months. I made two little dresses, plain enough for a boy or a girl, and a soft wool blanket. I didn't use the sewing machine; instead, I sewed all the seams by hand. All day, as I worked, I'd imagine leaving my chores to change the baby's diaper. In the evening, I heated extra water so

I'd have enough to bathe the baby. I heard it fussing in the morning, in the cradle Virgil would build for it to sit beside our bed, and dreamed I was rocking it to sleep every night. I thought how overjoyed Momma and Virgil would be when it finally came.

Only the baby didn't come to me. It came to Cate instead.

***

I hadn't seen her for months when she flounced into my kitchen, unexpected, and threw herself down at the table. I was standing by the stove, ironing, putting one iron on top of the stove to reheat as I ironed with the other.

"Damn it," she said.

"Cate," I said, annoyed, "you mustn't curse."

"I'm pregnant," she said, picking at her nails. When she came to us, they'd been long and elegant, but now they were short and ragged like a bad haircut.

"Why Cate, that's wonderful!" I said, but inside, I was stunned. Was this *my* baby, the baby I'd yearned for?

"What's so wonderful about it?"

"You want a baby, don't you? I'm thrilled for you!"

"Well, I'm not. Babies make you fat. I'm barely three months along and I already feel like a big, fat cow."

"But Cate," I said, "fat means nothing compared with having a baby. You'll get thin again afterward."

"How'll I keep my husband if I look like a pig?"

"He understands. Of course he understands. Isn't he thrilled?"

"You judge everything by how Virgil is. Gilly's not like that. He'll be disgusted."

"Disgusted? Doesn't he want a family? What did he say when you told him?"

"I haven't told him yet. I want to get rid of it, Sairy. I don't want a baby."

"Are you crazy? You can't do that," I told her. "What are you thinking? Cate, you're not right in your mind. Think about how lucky you are. Why, I'd give anything to have a baby."

"Well, it hardly matters. There's nothing I can do about it anyway." She fished around in her purse and pulled out a cigarette.

"You can't do that in here," I said. "Virgil won't stand for it."

"Oh...fine," she said, and threw it back into her purse without putting it back in the box.

"Cate, you'll feel different about this after you get used to it. Why don't you talk to Gilly about it? You'll see. He'll be happy, and then you'll be happier, too. Why, you'll be a real family now."

I ran to the bedroom and got the layette out of my drawer. "Look," I said, unfolding the clothes and laying them out on the table. "Look at these. Aren't they perfect? They're the most beautiful thing I've ever woven. I made them for the baby I wanted me and Virgil to have. But now, I'll give them to you. Your baby can have them. And I'll help you with it, Cate. You can leave it with us whenever you want. It'll be like my own baby, the baby I can't have."

"Oh, Sairy," she said, getting up and going over to the window so I couldn't see her face. "Everything's so simple to you."

Then she turned to face me, and her face clouded over. "How long have you been weaving those?" she asked me.

"Oh, quite a while," I said. "Four months, maybe."

"Four months. And I'm three months gone. This is *your* fault," she said, her voice tense with anger. "*You* did this."

"That's crazy talk. I was weaving these clothes for the baby I wanted for me and Virgil. Of course it had nothing to do with you getting pregnant."

She ran over to the kitchen counter and grabbed a paring knife. "Give me those right now," she said, reaching for the clothes.

I snatched them up from the table. "No!" I said.

"Get rid of them," she shrieked, "I'm cutting them up! Right now!"

"No! Stop it!" I hugged the clothes to my chest and started for the door. Cate ran behind me waving the knife, trying to take them from my hands. I ran outside, down the steps and toward Momma's house, tussling with Cate who, despite the fact I outweighed her by 10 or 15 pounds, was fighting like a wildcat to take the clothes out of my hands. When she couldn't get them away, she started slashing at them with the knife, trying to cut them up while I was still holding them.

"Cate, stop it! Get ahold of yourself," I shouted, dodging, trying to cover the weaving and getting nicked in the arm with the knife for my trouble. Turning my back on Cate, I wrapped my arms around the trunk of a big fir tree, holding the clothes between my body and the tree to keep Cate off of them. She tore at my dress and hair screaming bloody murder.

Suddenly, I heard Cate go "Ow!" and the frenzy at my back ceased. I turned back around to see Virgil wrestling with Cate. He had her wrists in his hands and was pulling her back toward the steps.

"That's enough," he said, looking as angry as I'd ever seen him.

"Virgil, watch out, don't be rough," I cried. "She's pregnant."

"I'm not going to hurt her," he promised, and then to Cate, "You settle down right now."

"Let me go!" she screamed, trying to drag one wrist up to her mouth so she could bite his hand.

Virgil forced her up the steps and onto the porch, where he made her sit down in my rocking chair. He kept hanging onto her wrists though, because she was now trying to claw at his face. When she realized she wasn't strong enough to fight him off, she lapsed into the chair and burst into hysterical tears.

"I hate you, you and that infernal loom," she cried. "Why did you do this to me?"

"Catie," I said, "I didn't do it." I dropped the clothes on the porch floor and knelt beside the rocking chair, stroking her face with my hands, willing her to be calm. "Honey, it'll be okay. Everything will be okay." She leaned into my shoulder and moaned and wept, rocking back and forth, inconsolable.

Momma came bustling onto the porch. She'd heard us shouting and come outside just in time to see Virgil take the knife away from Cate.

"You go on back to work," she told Virgil. "You don't need to be worrying about this when you're busy with more important things. Leave the women to take care of the women."

Virgil's face was still red with anger. He picked the knife up off the porch and went to put it away without saying a word.

"Now, what's all this about?" Momma said to Cate.

"I'm pregnant!" Cate cried. "I'm pregnant, and it's Sairy's fault!"

"Nonsense, child. Sairy didn't make you pregnant."

"She wove those clothes." Cate pointed to the heap of clothes. Momma eyed the clothes and gave me a look that said, "I told you no good would come of it." I should've been ashamed, but instead, my heart was singing with joy: my baby's coming.

"Sairy, go make us a cup of tea," Momma said. "And best take those clothes with you.

As I put the kettle on and got out the teapot, I heard Momma trying to soothe Cate. It took the two of us more than an hour and several pots of tea to coax her, if not into acceptance, at least into a display of dignity. She agreed to tell Gilly about the baby, too, and asked if she could call him from Momma's house.

"Shouldn't you tell him face-to-face?" Momma said.

"It'd be better this way," she said. "So you can be with me just in case."

"Just in case what?" I asked.

"Just in case anything."

We helped her over to Momma's house and got her a chair by the phone. She called, and I could hear Gilly's voice, loud and annoyed, punctuating their conversation, but couldn't make out the words.

"Hi, Honey...Yes, I'm over at Sairy's house...I know...I'm sorry...Well, how was I supposed to know you'd be back so early? You never are...Anyway, I've got something to tell you and I don't want you to get mad...What do you mean? You get mad about everything...Will you just shut up for a minute?...All right. Stop hollering. What I wanted to tell you was, I'm pregnant. I'm going to have a baby...What? Are you kidding me? Of course it is!...How dare you! Damn you to hell!" She slammed down the phone and crossed her arms over her chest. Tears started trickling down her cheeks again.

"Cate? What'd he say?" I asked. "He's not happy?"

"Oh just as happy as can be," she said sarcastically. "He had the nerve to ask me if it was his."

"He didn't!"

"Oh yes, he did."

"Why, that's just plain wicked! Cate," I said, suddenly feeling a stab of doubt, "he doesn't have any reason to think you've been unfaithful, does he?"

"Of course not. Don't you start in on me too, Sairy."

"Well, I just can't imagine why he would say such a thing."

"Because he's a big, mean-tempered jerk, that's why." Cate's voice rose, and it looked like she might be getting hysterical again.

"Now, now. Let's stop all this fussing," Momma intervened. "You need to worry about taking care of yourself and the baby and not get upset about a lot of silly nonsense from Gilly. He's just surprised, is all. You sit down and let me fix you a bite of supper."

As Momma bustled around the kitchen, Cate kept on talking. She told us she was jealous of Gilly, that she thought he was looking at other women. He criticized her, she said. He told her he'd put her in the nuthouse if she didn't straighten up. He said she was a slut and a slob.

It was probably then that I felt my first stirring of hatred for Gilly. I hated him for beating Cate down when she was so obviously fragile. I hated him for rejecting the child that was on the way – *my* child. Who understands the Lord's ways? Wouldn't Virgil and I have been better parents? We'd have brought it up in the Church and provided all the love any child could ever need. But as usual, I kept my thoughts to myself. It wouldn't do to criticize the husband in front of the wife. So I just listened and stored up the words in my heart. I began keeping a tally of Gilly's sins against Cate.

***

Contrary to Cate's expectation, she didn't get fat, at least not for a long time. She got thinner first, her face becoming pale and the bones sharp like little chips of rock under her white skin. Her shoulder bones stood out like wings and her wrists like frail, knobby twigs. She came over frequently, and I'd badger her with heaping plates full of biscuits and gravy, mashed potatoes dripping with butter, pork steaks swimming in fat, and anything else I thought might put some meat to her skeletal frame and nourish the baby growing inside.

The way she ate, I'm surprised the baby grew at all, but grow it did. Since Cate wouldn't eat, it sucked nourishment out of her flesh and bones. By the end of her term, she looked like a snake that'd swallowed a rat. Cate and Gilly kept going out honky-tonking until Cate didn't fit into any of her pretty clothes, and then Gilly went without her. She sat at home, brooding, or came to our place and rocked on Momma's porch. I assumed she'd get reconciled to the idea of having a baby, but as her pregnancy progressed, she complained without ceasing.

"I'm fat," she'd say.

"You're not fat. You're beautiful."

"I can't walk in my shoes. My feet are swelling."

"I'll lend you some better shoes. Those high heels aren't any good for a pregnant lady."

"I've got heartburn."

"Everyone gets heartburn when they're pregnant. Let me mix you up some soda."

"My figure's ruined."

"You're thin as a rail. Let me make you a pot roast."

"My back hurts."

"Put your feet up on this stool. I'll get you an aspirin."

"Gilly's out dancing with someone else."

"He is not. He's just out with his friends. He's married to the prettiest girl in the county, and now he's going to be a Daddy."

As Cate's due date approached, I looked forward to the birth with as much excitement as if it'd been my own. I wanted to hear about every gurgle, every kick and every twinge, thinking she might be going into labor.

"Leave that girl alone," Momma told me. "Stop hounding her about the baby. You're driving her crazy asking her every five minutes if she's having a pain. When the baby comes, she'll know it."

"Mrs. Fischer's daughter had her baby on the way to the hospital. She didn't even know she was in labor."

"Mrs. Fischer's daughter's had five children. This is different."

"Maybe she should stay with us until the baby comes. That way we'll be sure and get her to the hospital in time."

"Sairy, I was in labor with you twelve hours. Cate belongs at home with her husband."

But her husband didn't seem to care one way or another whether Cate was in labor. He left her alone all hours of the night without the car, never thinking how she'd get to the hospital without him. He never lifted a finger to help her, although he didn't work steady and had plenty of time on his hands. She looked worse and worse every time we saw her.

***

The baby finally came late one Thursday night. Momma got a phone call, threw on her robe and came running over to our place to roust Virgil and me out of bed. I met her downstairs, excited. The minute I heard her come in, I knew our baby was about to be born.

"Cate's in labor," she said. "She needs you and Virgil to take her to the hospital."

"Where's Gilly?" I demanded.

"She said he's gone," Momma said.

I ran back up the stairs. "Virgil, get up. We have to go take Cate to the hospital. The baby's coming."

"Where's Gilly?" he asked.

"She doesn't know. He took the car and left her alone."

Virgil just shook his head. He didn't approve of Cate, but he disapproved of Gilly even more. In Virgil's mind, a man had a sacred duty to his wife, to protect her and care for her no matter how flighty she was. Tired as he was after a full day's work, he rose without complaining to throw on some clean clothes and warm up the car.

It took us a half hour to get to Cate's house. When we arrived, all the lights were blazing, but the door was locked. Virgil knocked, and then, when he got no answer, began to pound and shout. I ran around the house looking in the windows…Cate was nowhere to be seen. I found a window that was unlatched, and asked Virgil to boost me inside. The house was cold and filthy and the floor littered with beer cans, cigarette butts and dirty dishes that'd been set down beside the couch. "Open the front door," Virgil called to me. "I don't want you alone in the house."

We went through the house opening doors, looking for Cate, and finally found her locked in the bathroom. We beat on the door until she opened it. She was sitting on the floor in a puddle of water with her back against the toilet, moaning and holding her belly. Virgil and I lifted her off the floor, sopped the water off her as best we could, and helped her out to the car.

"Where's your bag?" I said.

"I don't have one. Oh. Ooooooohhhhhh."

"Run in quick and throw a few things in a bag," Virgil said to me.

"No!" said Cate. "Get me to the hospital! Now! It hurts!"

I did what Virgil said. Cate's drawers were almost empty. They contained a few sweaters, most of them stained and snagged, and some flimsy underwear. I couldn't find her suitcase, but her nightgown was under the bed, so I shook it out and rolled it up with her toothbrush, hairbrush and underwear inside it, and ran back out to the car. Cate was panting and groaning and saying "Hurry, hurry!"

Virgil drove while I sat in the back with Cate, holding her hand and praying. I was scared the baby would come before we got there. After we arrived, though, it was hours before she finally gave birth. They whisked her right out of the car and into the back, and Virgil and I sat in the waiting room. They asked Virgil to sign some papers, and he said he couldn't do that; he wasn't her husband. So that made them ask where *was* her husband, and we had to say we didn't know. I thought maybe they wouldn't let Cate in because nobody was there to say they would pay for it, and I started crying, so Virgil put his arm around me and kissed the top of my head.

"Don't worry, Honey," he said. "They're not going to kick a woman having a baby out in the street."

Maybe they would've done that in the city, but in our little town they didn't. We waited for hours. They'd put magazines out for people to read while they waited, and I read some of those. Life in those magazines was surely puzzling. The women seemed to have every gadget and convenience you could imagine, and ought to have spent all their time sitting around with their feet up, but instead, they seemed to have all sorts of problems. The magazines told them how to fix their hair and put on their makeup and what they ought to wear for this occasion and that. Then, they had recipes and knitting patterns and helpful housekeeping hints like how to take coffee and lipstick stains out of a silk blouse.

"Why do they drink coffee in a silk blouse?" I wondered aloud, and Virgil said he figured they just put it in there to have something to write about.

"Don't get any foolish ideas," he warned, but he smiled, so I knew he was joking.

"How come I don't have silk blouses?" I demanded, and he promised he would get me one to milk the cows in.

I looked out the window and realize the sun had come up. I was starting to yawn my head off when the nurse finally came out and told us Cate'd had the baby.

"A little girl," she said. "Would you like to come see the Mama for a minute?"

Would we! You couldn't have torn me out of that hospital with a bulldozer. Poor Cate's hair was plastered to her head like dirty straw, and her eyes had dark circles around them. The pupils were larger than normal, so they looked dark instead of their usual sky-blue color.

"Cate!" I said, taking her limp hand. "How are you? How's the baby?"

"Okay, I guess," she said.

"Who does she look like?"

"Oh, I don't know," Cate said, and rolled her head sideways on the pillow like she didn't want to think about it.

Nowadays they hustle a woman right out of the hospital after she's had a baby, but Cate stayed five days. Not one time did Gilly come to see her. I, on the other hand, was down there every day, especially when it was time for Cate to feed the baby. She put it on the bottle. That's not what I would've done. But Cate said she wasn't going to nurse some old baby and ruin her figure.

When Cate got tired of holding her, which she generally did after a few minutes, she'd hand her over to me, and I'd sit and hold that baby until the nurse came and pried her out of my arms. Little Joleen had a bullet-shaped head, kind of pointy on top, and a heavy thatch of dark hair. The nurse said her head would flatten out in a few days, which it did, becoming round as a stone smoothed in the river. She screwed her little eyes shut tight and waved her hands wildly. When you plugged the bottle into her mouth, she'd stop waving and drink frantically, making a little glugging noise whenever she swallowed.

I guess I was the first person to lay eyes on Joleen excepting her mother and the doctor and nurse that were there when she was born. I saw her even before her own daddy. I asked Virgil to come to the hospital with me and see her, but he said he had to catch up on work. Now that I think back on it, I wonder if maybe it didn't hurt him to think that Gilly and Cate, who had no use for a baby, had one and we, who would've loved and cherished one, couldn't.

I drove Cate home from the hospital. I'd wanted her to come to our place, worried about leaving her in that house all littered with cigarettes and dirty plates, but she wanted to go home, wanted to find Gilly. He was home when we drove up, and he came to the door blinking and looking sleepy. Cate let me carry in the baby.

"Why aren't you at work?" Cate said to Gilly as she pushed past him into the house.

"Shut up."

"Who's gonna support this baby if you don't work?"

"Shut up, I said. Hey, where's the kid?" He reached out and brushed the blanket away from Joleen's face, then stared at her without interest.

"Hunh," he said. "Ugly kid. Looks nothin' like me." Then he turned into the house and bellowed at Cate, "Hey! Whose kid is this? It don't look nothin' like me."

Cate, white faced, appeared in the living room. "You know perfectly well it's yours."

I whipped around to put my body between Gilly and the baby. "You hush," I said. "Don't talk about this baby like that. She's your own daughter."

Gilly spat off the porch, then came in and shut the door. He lit a cigarette and stood looking at Cate. "This place is a pigsty," he said.

"You're the pig," she spat back at him. He raised his hand and moved toward her as if to slap her face, but I hollered right quick "Don't you two fight in front of the baby." At that, Gilly dropped his hand and went off into the back of the house.

"You sit down and hold Joleen," I told Cate. "I'm going to get this house cleaned up.

***

I got home late, worn out, still worried about Cate and the baby. Supper would've been late, but Momma'd come over and gotten my stove going.

"How's the baby?" she asked.

"Just precious," I said. "But Momma, Gilly doesn't even like that baby. He says she doesn't look anything like him."

"Babies never look like anyone, Momma said. Babies look like babies. What's wrong with that man?"

"I don't know, Momma. I think he's mean clear through. I cleaned up Cate's house this afternoon. It was a wreck."

"Sit on down, Sairy honey," said Momma. "I'll get this supper on." I sat down into one of our three chairs, sighed with relief to get off my feet and looked around the cabin. It was small and crowded with unmatched odds and ends of furniture, rag rugs, patchwork curtains made from scraps, and shelves crammed with canning jars, books, tools, dishes, pots and pans, and all the other accouterments of daily living. But it was neat and cozy, too. For all that Cate's house was bigger, I thought, and had hot and cold running water, I wouldn't trade it for this place in a million years. The cabin had me and Virgil and Momma imprinted on it like 'In God We Trust' was stamped on a coin.

"Go call Virgil in to wash up," Momma commanded. I went to the front porch and stood for a moment looking west to where the dark silhouette of the mountains stood flat against the burning sky. A jay flew overhead. Behind the cabin, the birch trees whispered in the evening breeze. I walked out to the front field where Virgil was mending fence and grabbed him around the chest, clinging to his back like a limpet.

"Come in for supper," I said into the hollow between his shoulder blades. He shook me off and turned around, then picked me up around the waist. He twirled me around and around under the trees, like we were dancing to the music of the sunset and the breeze in the birch trees.

"Okay," he said.

# Chapter 10

## ❧ Joleen ❧

Cate needed frequent breaks from Joleen. She'd call me up every few days and ask, "Can you sit with the baby? I need to get out of here." Sometimes she needed to go shopping, and sometimes she wanted to drive to Sandpoint, and sometimes she and Gilly wanted to go out of an evening. Those were my favorite times, because on those evenings, she'd leave Joleen with us all night and most of the next day.

I'd woven all those things for Joleen, but Cate flat refused to use them. The baby would wear nothing but store-bought, she said, no crummy old homemade for her. I kept on making things anyway, in secret, and when Joleen stayed all night, I'd dress her in one of the cotton frocks I'd made. They were as soft as a whisper, just right for Joleen's fragile baby skin. Now that I knew the baby was a girl, I'd dyed one dress with tea, a light beige color, and another one pink with Rit dye I bought at the dry goods store.

Joleen's dark hair had gotten longer, and fluffed out from her head like a bird's nest. I'd thread a ribbon through it and tie it around her head with a bow, and she'd look just as pretty as a Christmas present. While I cleaned up supper, Virgil would hold Joleen in his lap. She'd stand on his legs, as babies do, teetering and holding onto his fingers, bouncing up and down and flashing her toothless grin, just trilling away in rambling baby talk. As the months went by and she started rolling over, sitting up, cutting teeth and eating porridge, we thought of her more and more as our own. When I went to get her at Cate's house, she'd reach for me and start babbling, and I'd scoop her up and dance her around the room, blowing in her neck and singing silly baby songs with nonsense words.

"I don't even know why I bother with that girl," Cate would complain. "She likes you better than her own mother." Then she'd shrug and go fetch her strappy, high-heeled shoes from under the bed. "We won't be back until late," she'd say. "Don't let the baby drool on me." She'd stand at a distance and kiss the air an inch over Joleen's head so she wouldn't get baby cereal on her nice sweater. Then she'd be out the door and gone.

I'd go through the house gathering up all Joleen's dirty diapers, picking up her little dresses and socks from the floor, and collecting all her slimy bibs and milk-filmed bottles. Then I'd pile them all in a canvas sack and tote them out to the car. Momma and I would trade off playing and rocking with Joleen and washing all the dirty things, boiling the bottles, make sure everything was sweet and clean for our girl.

"You're not her maid," Virgil would grumble when he saw us stirring a pot of simmering diapers or boiling bottles.

"It's for Joleen," I'd protest. "The girl needs clean diapers. She'll get sick drinking out of dirty bottles."

"Let them do it," he'd frown. "What else have they got to do?"

Virgil could act as huffy as he wanted...I knew he loved Joleen like his own child. When she started trying to walk, that stage where babies totter around holding onto the furniture, he'd attach her to his leg, stand her on his foot and let her grab him around the calf, then stump around the house singing "I'll Fly Away" while Joleen shrieked with laughter. When she stayed weekends, he'd take her out driving on the tractor and introduce her to the goats and the cows.

"She'll be a good little stockman," he said. He let her name all the animals, even the chickens, and listened to her gravely when she insisted that none of them be slaughtered, not even if we had to go hungry. We slaughtered only when she was with her Mama and Daddy. When she asked where Boo Boo was or Kathy or Hooter, we'd say "She (or he) went to live at the chicken nursing home."

"I want to go visit," she'd say.

"It's too far away," Virgil would say, "all the way over in Wyoming."

Fortunately, she was young enough so we could distract her with a new lamb or chick, and she'd forget all about the old ones. Over time, the chicken nursing home became an elaborate facility for old animals of every stamp, including wild birds that fell from the nest and couldn't be salvaged, and even an occasional frog that Joleen brought in from the spring and housed in a canning jar. They had radios there, we said, that played only animal news and The Happy Farmer, and beds of swans' down and hot mash for animals with no teeth.

Maybe we were wrong to lie to her, I fretted, but Momma was philosophical about it. No sense upsetting the child, she said. She'll have plenty of time to learn the hard facts of life without throwing them in her face when she's a baby. I wondered where all this sentiment had been when Danny and I were little. She'd never allowed us to shirk the truth, no matter how ugly.

When Joleen turned four, she wanted a kitten, and badgered us for one relentlessly. Momma'd never been a pet person, said we didn't have money to feed useless mouths, so I'd never had an animal in the house except occasionally a box of new baby chicks she'd keep behind the stove for a day or two until they were strong enough to stand the springtime chill. But we could refuse Joleen nothing. Even Momma made no demur when Virgil found a tiny kitten sitting in a box downtown in front of the Visitor Center and brought it home in his pocket. He sat Joleen down in a kitchen chair and made her close her eyes, then put the kitten in her lap and said, "You can open them now." Joleen shrieked and hugged the kitten so hard Virgil had to rescue it so it didn't get squashed. "You have to be gentle with baby things," he said, and showed her how to tickle it behind the ears and under the chin until it made a tiny rattling noise. "It's purring," he explained. "That means it's happy."

Joleen name the kitten Holly, but Virgil called it Holy Terror. When Joleen wasn't around, it would get bored and knock things off the shelves or chew on the hems of the curtains. When I walked past, it would climb up my leg inside my dress, make me feel like my flesh was getting raked with a thousand needles. I'd hop around the house batting at the kitten under my dress and hollering "Get down from there, you!" and Virgil would laugh to beat the band.

Joleen wanted to take the kitten home with her, but Cate wouldn't have it. "It's got fleas," she said, and brushed it contemptuously out of her way with her strappy shoe.

"No she doesn't," said Joleen, starting to pout. She had a will of iron, our Joleen, even at the age of four.

"Don't sass your mama," I said hastily, not wanting the kitten subjected to Gilly and Cate's unreliable care. "You leave Holly here. You're up here all the time. You can play with her when you come see us." Joleen clouded up and looked like she might pitch a fit, but Virgil put a stop to it. He had an authoritative way about him for all his gentleness, and he could do a lot more to control Joleen than me or Momma, either one.

Truth tell, Holly comforted us those nights when Joleen was at home with her real folks. I'd take the old thread spool I'd tied to a string and drag it across the floor, and Holly would chase after it, thinking it was a mouse, maybe, until she caught it, rolled over on her back and raked it with her back claws while holding it between her front feet.

Joleen outgrew the layette I'd woven almost before I'd sewn the last stitch. That didn't worry me. I was always busy at the loom, every minute I had spare from chores, and it was always something for Joleen. By this time, I could weave a beautiful web: stripes or even herringbone, just as good as a four-harness floor loom. It was slow, of course. But I liked that things of beauty could come from nothing more than a pile of old sticks.

I was careful not to let Joleen wear anything I made her back to her own house, even when she wanted to. "These are special clothes just for Aunt Sairy's house," I told her. I made her dresses in bright colors: red, green, blue and yellow. And for church, white ones with tatted lace around the sleeves and collar. It was glorious, everything I'd dreamed of, to have my own child. My only grief was that she had to go back to her parents – her blood parents, I thought of them. We were her real parents.

***

Right around this time, Danny got married to Shella, a girl he'd met over in Tacoma where he went to live after he got out of school. As Momma predicted, Danny'd gone to college. He spent four years in Boise getting his degree, and then he moved over to the coast. While he was down in Boise, he'd come back home every summer, but after he moved to Tacoma, we hadn't seen him for several years.

Tacoma was a long way off. Momma didn't like that Danny'd moved so far away, but she'd gotten more resigned to it after Virgil came and took the place she'd wanted for Danny, getting the land in order. She was happy Danny was educated and working an educated man's job.

"Farming and logging's a hard life," she said. "Look at your Daddy and your Grampy, dying young the way they did.

Better for Danny to work in the city. You live longer sitting behind a desk. I wish he'd find something closer to home, is all."

I guess she missed Danny more than she let on, because when she heard about the wedding, she complained. "I don't even know this girl's family. Why couldn't he find a nice girl from around here?"

"A man marries where he lives," Virgil said, and as usual, Momma agreed with him.

"Lord, forgive me for complaining," she said. "I don't know what's gotten into me."

"You miss your boy, is all, Momma," Virgil said, giving her a comforting pat. "My Mama went through the same thing when I got married, said she didn't know what to do with herself now her son was a grown man with a wife of his own."

"The man shall leave his mother and father and cleave to his wife," Momma said as if to convince herself. "It's God's way."

I understood Danny's choice, as Momma couldn't. She hadn't been a laughing stock at school all those years with our threadbare clothes and country ways. And Danny wasn't strong. He got picked on for being scrawny and delicate among the robust sons of farmers and mill workers. He'd been right to move away. In the big city, he could get a fresh start with people who didn't know he was a hick. Maybe the office workers and lawyers and such didn't look down on pale, skinny Danny. I didn't say this to Momma, though, because I didn't want to hurt her feelings. She'd done as best she could for us.

***

The three of us traveled to Tacoma on the train for the wedding. We stayed two nights in a motel over there, and I took about six baths in those two days just to revel in the luxury of running a tub full of steaming water without hauling one bucket. I finally had to unlock the door so Momma and Virgil could use the bathroom while I was in the tub because up until then, they kept hollering and beating on the door for me to get out of the dad gum bath tub before they all burst apart at the seams.

Danny came to pick us up at the train station, but Shella, his wife-to-be, wasn't with him. She was getting her dress fitted, Danny said, and other last-minute preparations for the wedding. Besides, he wanted us to himself for an evening. He took us out to dinner at a restaurant, where he had to order for us because we didn't understand what the food was. Italian, he called it, and it tasted good. I had little dough pouches filled with cheese in a pale sauce, and Virgil had noodles covered with canned tomatoes. Momma ordered the same thing Danny was eating, which he said was chicken. It didn't look like any chicken parts I'd ever seen, and I thought I knew everything there was to know about chickens. It was all smothered in gravy of some sort, and Momma said it tasted strange, but it was good.

The restaurant was dark and there were candles on the tables, so we sat in our own little glowing bubble and listened to the hum of conversation from the little bubbles around the other tables. How can you see your food, Momma wondered, but Danny referred to it as "ambiance".

Danny seemed happy. He told us how he and Shella had met at an office party, and how he'd slowly worked up the nerve to ask her out. He seemed relieved that she'd consented to marry him, like he wasn't good enough for her. This wounded Momma, who thought the sun rose and set over Danny's head. Shella's a lucky girl, she kept saying to him, patting his hand and marveling at how sophisticated he was now.

It turned out the bathtub was the best part of the city. It was so noisy we couldn't get to sleep, with cars and buses and streetcars roaring past all day and night. When you walked outside at night, you couldn't see the stars. The lights of the city, which came on at sunset and went off after sunrise, blotted them out. Everyone but us seemed as busy as ants on a dead carcass, but nobody was carrying groceries or laundry or anything that looked important enough to bring about such a tizzy. They mostly seemed to spend their time hurrying from one place to another as if the world would wither away if they weren't in the right spot at exactly the right minute.

The next afternoon, we dressed in our nicest Sunday clothes and went to the wedding. Danny was too busy to pick us up so he had one of Shella's uncles take us. Shella turned out to be a nice enough girl. We all felt rough around her and her family; they had a town polish that made us feel like bumpkins. Every time we said something that revealed our provincial origins, they'd get real quiet and raise their eyebrows to each other like they didn't want to be rude but couldn't help feeling appalled at what a family of rubes their precious little girl was marrying into. You could almost see them resolving not to let the grandchildren spend too much time alone with their country grandma. Even Virgil, who generally exuded quiet confidence, seemed ill at ease. Nobody admired the verdant, productive little slice of Paradise he'd made of our property; only Danny showed any curiosity about the place.

Shella was full of stories about Danny's successes, his "rising star" as she called it, with the firm he was working for. I couldn't quite figure out what they did, auditing they called it. It had to do with banking, I supposed. Numbers were never my strong suit, and Danny's either, so it surprised me to hear what a great name he was making for himself. He sat silent through most of her effusions, blushing every now and then, patting her knee and throwing in an awkward word about how it wasn't really such a big deal. She was full of plans about houses in town and automobiles and private schools for the children. She seemed eager to emphasize that Danny was part of her world, now, a far cry from the simple country boy he'd been raised as.

Danny was looking harassed and unhealthy, though maybe that was just the strain of the wedding. Momma started out making comments about how he needed a good, home-cooked meal of vegetables from the garden, well water and meat right off the farm, but this brought on a round of raised eyebrows and significant glances so she kept quiet about it after that.

The wedding didn't happen in a church, but in some sort of hall that was part of a club Shella's mother belonged to. Momma wasn't too happy about that. We all sat at a table together at the reception watching the dancing because we didn't know the steps and sipping fruit punch because none of us would try the champagne. Danny and Shella twirled around the floor together, and I must say, she looked like a vat of whipped cream in her frothy white gown. They smiled into each other's eyes and I thought, they'll be all right.

That was the last time we saw Danny alive. There were to be no grandchildren to put through private school or keep away from their hick grandma, as it turned out. I was glad to have that memory of him and his whipped-cream bride spinning around the floor like a fairy princess and her prince, so happy and full of promise.

Danny and Shella left for a honeymoon right after the reception, so the same uncle that brought us to the wedding drove us back to the train station the next morning. Before that, though, Virgil and Momma and I went for a ride on the streetcar. We were used to getting up early, so we rose when the sun was barely tingeing the city gray. We hopped on the car right outside the motel room and rode downtown and back again, watching the busy people getting on and off, never speaking or looking at each other. The sheer size of it overwhelmed me, the tall buildings with their rows of windows mostly dark at this hour of the morning, the giant buses and the endless miles of concrete and asphalt and steel ribbons of streetcar tracks. Virgil hated the noise and the cigarette smoke that permeated the atmosphere everywhere, even on the streetcar. I found it exciting, if exhausting. No wonder Danny wanted to stay. I might have been tempted myself if it wasn't for Virgil and Joleen.

\*\*\*

Cate and Gilly were to have tended the stock while we were away, but it turned out they hadn't bothered. The animals were hungry and in pain from not being milked. It was only one of a handful of times I saw Virgil really angry.

"We're not going away again," he vowed. "Good thing it was only two days or we'd have a lot of dead animals on our hands."

Holly met us at the door in a flurry of delight, mewing and winding around under our feet so I almost fell into the stove tripping over her. The house was cold and unwelcoming, and I made haste to build a fire and cozy it up again. I couldn't bear the bleak feeling of a house with no fire. It felt like a body with no heart.

Virgil was on the phone to Cate, complaining about the stock and being told that Gilly'd gone on a drunk and no way was Cate going to ruin her hands messing with animals. Momma went home to light her own fire, and later, we gathered for a companionable supper of reheated lamb stew and dumplings. I fed Holly the scraps of stew, walked onto the porch and looked up at the sky to see a million jewels scattered across the heavens and the pale wash of the Milky Way painted on the black sky. The excitement of the city, even the glories of a bathtub, couldn't compare with this.

\*\*\*

It was only a few months later that Momma got the call about Danny and Shella being killed in an automobile accident.

They'd been driving to Olympia, Shella's mother wept into the phone, when a truck crossed the middle line and ran into them head-on. There was nothing left of the car but a mashed-up pile of scrap, and not much left of Danny and Shella, either.

All I could think about was Danny and me in our little loft bedroom, skating across the floor on our rag rug. Danny wearing his lumpy hat down to the school bus and then tucking it into his pocket so he wouldn't get teased by the other kids. Danny getting his foot stuck under a rock in the middle of the river, and Virgil coming to our rescue like a prince in a fairy tale. Danny on the dance floor with Shella in her creamy dress, smiling into his eyes. And me, jealous of Danny, Momma's golden boy, and wishing her eyes would light up over me like they did when she smoothed down his cowlick and kissed the top of his head.

That was when I started to get an inkling that having your dreams come true might be a mixed blessing. Had I wished this on him, I wondered, when I yearned to crowd him out of Momma's heart? Had he remained half-formed, a shadow of a person, because my dreams of importance kept him from solidifying into a material man, a man with enough substance, enough gravity, to make a permanent hole in the fabric of time? Worse yet, did my dreams cause him to be excised from Momma's life as he couldn't be from her heart?

Joleen, who's studied psychology and other modern ideas, says this type of envy, and its accompanying guilt, are common among siblings. But Joleen hasn't seen the bitter fruit of the dream-weaver's art. I've not told her the story I'm telling you.

***

Momma and I took the train to Tacoma again for the funeral. Virgil stayed home this time to look after the stock. The city was as gray and noisy as before, but the excitement was all gone out of it like the juice sucked out of an orange. It looked dull and sordid. The busyness of its inhabitants seemed pathetic, like they were trying to distract themselves from the gritty futility of their surroundings by moving fast. Momma and I stayed awake most of the night reading from the scriptures, how we are not to grieve like those who have no hope, and we tried to comfort each other.

Momma wanted to bring Danny home, but she gave in to Shella's mother, who wanted them buried together in Tacoma, and told her in gusty sobs that she couldn't have her daughter so far away from her. Momma swallowed her own pain and let Shella's mother have her way. It was the Christian thing to do, she said.

As an 84-year-old woman, I've attended plenty of funerals, including my husband's, my mother's and my best friend's. When you reach my age, life starts to seem like a long sentence of time segmented by the punctuation marks of death. Before Danny's death, I was an innocent dreamer. Danny's passing woke me up to the inevitable consequences of meddling with people's lives. I guess it isn't really true that Danny's death woke me up to the consequences. It started waking me up. It was another death that truly put the period on my innocence.

I'm not sure Momma ever completely recovered from losing Danny. However, being the matter-of-fact person she was, she picked herself up and carried on. I remember the very day we returned from the funeral, she turned out all her cupboards and scrubbed shelves late into the night, tossing dusty old junk in the burn pile and putting back the rest all neat and organized. Maybe she was determined to wipe the past clean, keep only the things that would help her meet the rest of her life head-on.

"Let the dead bury their dead," she said. "We've got the living to worry about."

It used to be that at rest, her face retained a focused tension that made it look determined and a little grim. After the funeral though, when she wasn't thinking about anything in particular, it would settle into soft, wistful folds, sagging a little from the jowls and giving her an aging, sorrowful appearance.

I asked her about it once or twice. Did she miss Danny something awful? And she said yes and no. She missed him; it wasn't natural to outlive your children. And at the same time, it was a relief she had no worries about him any more; her job as a mother was forever complete. I found this answer unsatisfying. Even with Danny gone I still could envy him.

"What about me?" I said. "Don't you still have me to worry about?"

And she replied "Oh, Sairy. I always knew you'd be all right. You were always the strong one." Me. The strong one. I protested against the idea, not out loud but in my own mind, thinking I was no more than a blade of grass under the mower. But now, I know her mother's heart saw things clearer than I. I had depths of stubborn willfulness she saw and I denied.

Danny died in early November. It made for a sorrowful winter. Winters are long and gray in Idaho, and particularly the time of year before the snow comes to bury everything in blinding cleanliness. The fields are brown, the birch and aspen woods naked and broken. Everything's drearier at that time, and losing Danny made it seem more so.

We tried to rally for Thanksgiving, inviting Cate, Gilly and Joleen over for a feast. Gilly brought a jug of wine along. Momma met him at the door and ordered him to take it right back to the car; he wasn't going to bring liquor into the house. Gilly looked like he might run right over Momma, but Virgil came up behind her and told him that's right, he wasn't setting foot in his house with liquor. At that, Gilly's face turned red and he roared at Cate and Joleen to get back in the car, they weren't eating at any Bible thumper's house. Joleen started to cry and Cate slapped her, which darn near sent Virgil off the porch and over to the car to do Lord knows what to Cate, except Momma grabbed his arm and whispered in his ear and he just stomped back into the house. We ate the feast just among the three of us, but it wasn't the same without Joleen. The joy had been sucked out of the day.

I was fearful Gilly and Cate might keep Joleen away from us after that, but they didn't. Cate ignored us for a week, but then she wanted to go chasing Gilly around to the bars again and had no one else to watch her, so back she came just as always. I told Joleen tales of the big city, about riding on the streetcar and watching the people bustling around, and she said that's where she wanted to live when she grew up. I told her watch out what you wish for because her Mama'd been to the city and it could chew a person up and spit them back out all mangled, but that just made her want it worse. She badgered Cate to tell her what it was like until Cate told her to shut up, the city was a bad place for a woman alone and she wouldn't talk about it.

\*\*\*

When Joleen was in first grade, Virgil got injured when the tractor rolled over on him while he was driving it sideways on the hill. One leg got crushed beneath the tractor and we had quite a time getting him out. We called on the pastor, who called on a neighbor who brought a winch to set the tractor upright, but Virgil's leg was broken in three places. He was laid up for weeks, and Momma and I had to tend to everything on the place, quite a job for two women, one of them not so spry as she used to be.

It irritated Virgil to be sedentary. He could see the place going to rack and ruin, he said, with only two women to keep it going. This offended me, as I figured Momma and I managed just fine before we knew him, and I said so. It was the first time he and I truly argued. I was tired trying to do all my chores and all his, too, and I fussed at him when he would badger me about all the minutest details of the stock.

"Those animals aren't going to die in the next two months," I'd say when he grilled me about such and such a pregnant goat or this or that cow's milk production, or the weight the beef cattle were putting on. "Goats've been having kids for a hundred years without a vet. We can't afford a vet with you laid up," I declared.

Then he flared up at me, said I had no head for business and I should be more interested in the animals that put food on the table than a bunch of silly housework. He even criticized me for spending too many hours weaving, said we could buy fabric for a buck a yard and weaving was a needless expense. We should spend the money getting the cattle inoculated, he said, instead of wasting money on fripperies. I retaliated by spending my entire butter-and-egg money on yarn.

I complained to Momma and Cate, and neither of them gave me any sympathy. Momma told me to straighten up and treat my husband with respect, and Cate snorted and said I didn't have much to put up with; I should try living with *her* husband. Instead of bringing me to my senses, these comments made me resentful. I decided Virgil didn't appreciate me the way he should and I was going to make him admit my work was just as important as his. So I became even more lackadaisical about tending the stock and let my chores slip, too. I figured if he went without good food and clean laundry for a while, he'd come around. Instead, he bore it in stubborn silence. He stopped asking about the stock and ate whatever I fixed without comment.

After several weeks, Virgil was able to hobble around with a cane, but he'd missed the second hay cutting and the crop, when he did bring it in, was practically worthless. Consequently, we had to buy hay for the stock that winter, which we couldn't afford, and our money troubles continued for almost the next year.

I'd never paid much attention to our finances. I didn't spend much, of course, because I was raised without any money to spend. Things'd gotten easier in the years since Virgil started managing the place, but our ways were still frugal. Now, I left it to Virgil to do all the fretting and scrimping and simply carried on as usual, refusing to be interested in how Virgil was going to make ends meet until we could start feeding the stock off our own place again. Momma gave me a dry look every now and then, as if to say wasn't I acting like a spoiled brat, but I ignored her, too.

For months, Virgil and I hardly spoke except when Joleen was over, to pretend everything was normal. We slept with our backs to each other. It wasn't long before I started missing him. My anger only lasted for a week or so, but I was prideful and wasn't about to make the first move toward peace. Virgil, though quiet, was his own kind of stubborn, and I guess he wasn't willing to apologize, either. The companionable suppers and idyllic lunches in the field together were over. I'd send Momma out with a sandwich or just wait for Virgil to show up and root through the pantry for something to eat.

The Lord only knows how long we would've carried on this foolishness if something hadn't intervened. What happened was, one day early the next summer, when Virgil had been out mending fence in the back field, he came running to the door shouting "Sairy, get on the phone to the hospital, quick!" Turned out one of the neighbors' nephews visiting from Spokane had fallen into the pond and nearly drowned before Virgil happened on him. He'd dragged him out onto the bank and cleared the water out of his lungs, pounding on his back until he took a choking breath. Momma ran down the road and fetched his parents, and I called an ambulance to carry him to the hospital.

The boy was okay, but the incident reminded me that life can vanish in an instant, and I had to stop worrying about who was right and wrong and make up with Virgil while I still had him. I cooked his favorite meal that night, and before I served it, I knelt by his chair, leaned my head against his arm and told him I couldn't bear living without him no matter how ornery he was. He put his arm around me and rubbed his bad leg and said he guessed we were both as ornery as old cow pies so maybe we deserved each other. And that's how we made up.

To celebrate, Virgil took me to my first real movie. The movie was called State Fair, and that fair certainly was cleaner than any fair I ever went to. Virgil said that's the way movies are; folks don't want to see all the dirt that happens in real life. They can just look outside their window to see that, he said. When they go to the movies, they want things to have a little polish on them. Well, we had a wonderful time. We ate popcorn and drank lemonade even though money was tight and we couldn't really afford it, and we leaned against each other when the romantic parts came. I even slipped my hand into Virgil's because it was dark and nobody could see us.

The next morning Momma told us she was relieved we'd come to our senses and she hoped there would be no more nonsense. I promised her there wouldn't be, and there never has been. Even near the end, when Virgil couldn't work or even rise from his bed for two years, we never fussed like that again. He didn't snipe at me about weaving or housework, and I did my best to manage as he would've done. He walked with a limp for the rest of his life, and on cold mornings, his bones in that leg would pain him. It was a reminder that love has to be tended like stock or it won't stay healthy.

# Chapter 11

## ✥ Cate and Gilly, Part 2 ✤

These years with us all together: Momma, Virgil and Joleen, were like a song in three-part harmony, but with Cate in the picture, we couldn't go too long without discord.

"Sairy, I have to see you." Cate's voice on the phone that morning was agitated.

"Is this about Joleen?" I asked. Lately I'd been letting Joleen wear the things I made her to school. It seemed that over the years, Cate'd forgotten about her refusal to let Joleen wear homemade things. Money was always tight at their house, since Gilly never worked steady, and I think it was a relief not having to worry about Joleen's clothes on top of everything else. We made sure Joleen ate hearty, and had decent clothes to wear to school, and Gilly and Cate worried only about themselves. But now, I was afraid she would be angry with me for going against her wishes.

"No, it's not about Joleen," Cate said. "It's about me. Let me come over."

"Of course you can come over," I said. "Why don't you wait 'til Joleen's out of school and bring her with you? You-all can have supper with us."

"I don't want to wait," she said. "Can't you think about anyone but Joleen?"

"I'm sorry," I said, immediately repentant, and feeling not a little guilty for being such a lackadaisical friend, "Come on over, then. I'll call the school and tell them to put Joleen on the bus to our place instead of sending her home."

"I'll be there in half an hour," Cate said. "And listen, Sairy...I need to talk to you alone, okay? We can send Joleen over to your Momma's. Virgil isn't there, is he?"

"Well of course he's here," I said. "But he's out working right now. I'm just wringing out the laundry; I'll get that hung up before you get here."

Cate had gotten harder over the years. She'd taken to wearing tighter clothes and higher heels, but not elegant like when she first came from the city. Her things were cheap and poorly made, puckered at the seams and the sweaters pilling from wear. That day, she wore a tight, wool skirt that was shorter than I liked, revealing her knees, without stockings, and a short jacket with no buttons over a tight blouse. Her lipstick was apple red, matching her too-bright rouge, and she wore blue makeup around her eyes. Her face was brittle and lined. She looked like an eggshell that might shatter at any second. She came teetering up the steps in her ridiculous heels, which she insisted on wearing even though she knew they were impossible to walk in on our gravel drive.

"Ugh," she said, examining one heel. "This driveway is ruining my heels. Why don't you get it paved?"

"We don't need the expense, honey," I said. "Why do you wear your nice shoes out here when you know the gravel scrapes them to pieces?"

"Oh, never mind that," she said. "Let's go inside. There's something I need you to do for me."

"Will you have some lemonade?" I offered.

"Ugh. I hate that stuff. Don't you have any coffee?"

"Sure. Let me put it on." I stepped onto the back porch, where the summer stove was, checked to see if the fire was still smoldering, and put a pot of cold coffee from breakfast on.

"Now," I said, sitting across the table from Cate, "Tell me what on earth is going on."

Cate picked at the table with her thumbnail. "It's Gilly," she said. "He's – he's taken up with another woman." Her face flushed pink. "Some whore," she added.

"Cate, don't talk like that. How do you know he's taken up with someone else?"

"I caught him," she said.

It turned out Cate had taken to following Gilly around to see where he went. He and she had always done a lot of drinking, but they mostly did that together after Joleen was born. Lately, he'd started going out on his own more and more, and Cate had gotten suspicious. She'd borrowed the neighbor's car and gone searching for him at all the places they liked to go together. Usually, she couldn't find him at any of those places, but last night had been different. She'd found his car at one of their favorite spots and gone barreling in to discover Gilly on the dance floor with another girl.

"He was dancing with someone else?" I said. "In public? A married man?"

"Yes, Sairy. In public. A married man. With someone else."

I didn't see why Cate was being sarcastic. Surely she was as shocked as I was, or why would she be here? I tried to think why Gilly might've been dancing with someone else, besides the adultery Cate obviously suspected, but I couldn't see any other reason for it.

"Still," I said, "You don't know they've actually— done anything, do you?"

"I most certainly do," she said. "If you'd seen the way they were dancing, you'd know, too."

"Well, I'm sorry for you, Cate, honey. He surely should not be doing a thing like that. I do wish you-all had a pastor that could talk to him about it."

"Is that all you have to say?"

"Well, what do you want me to say? What's to be done? Do you think his parents know? Do you – do you want Virgil to talk to him?"

"No, Sairy, I don't want Virgil to talk to him. Like that would do any good. I want *you* to help me. You have to help me end this. I want my husband back."

Honestly, I couldn't see why. Gilly had never been anything but a poor excuse for a husband. But I guess any wife has her pride. No one wants to be made a laughing stock or, worse yet, an object of pity all over town because her husband's carrying on with another woman right under her nose.

"Cate, what can I possibly do to help with that? Gilly would never listen to me. Even if he would, I would never dare say anything to him."

"I don't want you to talk to him, Sairy," she said. "I want you to make him come back to me. Weave something. Make that woman drop dead, or break out in hives, or come down with something awful. I want my husband back."

"Cate, I can't do that," I protested.

"Oh really?" she said. "I bet you'd do it for Virgil."

She had me there. I *would* do it for Virgil. In fact, I'd done it for every, single thing I wanted really badly. If I thought I was going to lose Virgil, I couldn't have helped myself. I'd have sat down at the loom without even wanting to, and as I wove, an image would fill my head and get woven into the web without any decision on my part. Cate must've seen these thoughts cross my face, because she tapped her fingers impatiently on the table and said "Well?"

I tried to put her off. I would've rather woven a volcano rising out of my own living room than put Gilly and Cate back together to torment each other. "You know I don't believe in this," I told her. "I think you're wasting your time. You need to be thinking about other ways to handle this."

"Sairy, I know you can help me," she said. "You have to help me. You want me to be happy, don't you?"

I did want Cate to be happy. I couldn't forget what she'd been to me all those years, the magical friendship of our childhood that'd set me free from being an outcast. Before her, I'd had nobody. I was untouchable. After she came, we had our self-contained society of two, and the whole rest of the world could go to Hades in a hand basket for all it mattered to us.

"All I can promise is to try," I warned her. "Please don't count on this working."

"It'll work," she said. "It has to."

It was the third time I'd ever sat down to the loom with a particular goal in mind. The first time, I'd woven Danny's hat, and that hadn't worked like I wanted it to. It hadn't worked like I *thought* I wanted it to. The second time was for Joleen, and though I couldn't be sorry about doing it, that hadn't worked exactly the way I thought it would, either. Mostly, though, the dreams had presented themselves unasked for, and my fingers worked of their own volition to weave them into whatever depth of reality they might take.   This was different. I couldn't muster any enthusiasm for it, and my dreams were always clearest when fueled by passion. But Cate was so adamant. She was so angry. What would she do if I said no? Kill the woman? Stop loving me?

I told myself that it surely must be the right thing to bring husband and wife back together. God didn't countenance adultery. Surely it was right, and not wrong, to do everything in my power to restore Cate's marriage. And, if God had given me the ability to weave things into being, then I could use that to bring about a good result. Such was my rationalization for taking Cate's situation into my hands.

The doing was harder than I anticipated. First, I had to conjure firmly into my mind the thing I was trying to weave. I rejected Cate's idea of bringing down disaster on the other woman's head. That didn't seem right. Gilly was guilty, too; why should she pay the whole price?

It took me a while to come up with something that seemed appropriately moral. I tried to envision Gilly as the perfect husband, but his real character, drunken and loutish, kept obtruding on the picture. So then I tried to envision him penitent. "I'm sorry," his mouth said, but his face was angry and bored, self-justifying. Finally, I had to settle for a picture of the two of them standing beside one another hand in hand and the other woman off to the side and behind, not getting in the way of their partnership. Then I sat down to weave. At Cate's suggestion, I wove a small piece to cover the cushion in Gilly's favorite chair, a wing chair and matching footstool that stood in Cate's living room, usually surrounded by empty, reeking beer cans and cartons of take-out chicken.

The color was deep brown, which I thought of as a steadfast color, the color of promise and fulfillment, the color of earth that brings forth fruit. The material was stout cotton, strong and hard-wearing. I struggled to keep my mind on Cate and Gilly as I wove, but as I did, Joleen crept into my thoughts. She looked solemn, gazing up at them as if pleading for an equal share of attention while they stared straight ahead. Nor did they notice one another. They seemed utterly submerged in their own internal mechanisms, nurturing their resentment as it blossomed into nightmarish flowers of hatred. Each time these thoughts arose, I pushed them firmly aside. I painted smiles on their faces. I forced them to turn and look at each other, to gather Joleen in with loving arms.

I didn't realize that some dreams, like the dreams of love I had about Momma, Virgil and Joleen, had their root in real love. This love could be fanned to a blaze because the embers were there awaiting the vivifying stream of oxygen my dreams provided. In Cate and Gilly, no such embers existed. Their hearts were piles of cold ash.

Still, I wove the best dream I could muster. I wove with feverish intensity. It was painful to keep my mind on Cate and Gilly. Their rancor infected me, and the brown thread took on a rancid, filthy aspect that seemed to fill the house with the noxious miasma of hatred. Even Virgil, usually the least fanciful of men, noticed it.

"What is that you're working on?" he asked. "It's the ugliest thing you've ever made."

"It's for Cate," I said.

"Why would she want that ugly thing?"

"It's not supposed to be ugly," I said helplessly. "It just turned out that way."

Cate didn't find it ugly. She came over almost daily to watch it take form and gloated over it, spewing a poison stream of invective against Gilly and his other woman as I beat the muddy threads in place.

"Stop it, Cate," I told her. "I can't work with you talking like that. I feel like there's spiders crawling all over my skin."

She'd go outside on the porch, then, silent but still enveloped in a cloud of cigarette smoke and indignation. When I'd finished it, I folded it into a square, sewed it up and stuffed it with the innards of the old pillow Cate provided, reeking of cigarette smoke and gray with unfulfilled longing. Cate seized the pillow and carried it triumphantly home as if bearing her vindication.

She put it on his chair and waited for the result, gnawing her already ragged fingernails even shorter. Meanwhile, she continued to pursue Gilly with relentless fury through the town, haunting the dance halls for glimpses of him and the other woman, projecting daggers of rage at the two of them, but mostly at her, reviling her as a witch, a temptress, a conniving harpy. Every couple of days she'd call me up and complain.

"It's not working. He was out with her again last night."

"Leave him be, Cate. You aren't helping yourself by following them around."

"I can't leave him be. Why isn't anything happening? You messed it up on purpose. You don't want him to come back to me."

"I did the best I could. Maybe God doesn't want you two back together."

"Hush up. I don't want to hear about your old God. If you can make a baby, you can fix a marriage."

You might've thought Cate would have more time for Joleen since she and Gilly were estranged, but she was too busy with her maniacal crusade to get him back (or bring him down, I wasn't sure which was the most important to her). Joleen came over every day after school. I was glad, not only for my sake and Virgil's, but because it seemed to lift Momma's melancholy as well. She and Momma would make tea and cookies, and take some out to Virgil at his work.

"Why don't you bring over some of your friends?" I asked her. "You could play out in the woods together." I was thinking of the magical days Cate and I'd spent roaming through those woods together. I wanted Joleen to have those days.

"I don't have any friends, Auntie Sairy," she said, crumpling up her nose in a little pouty face.

"Well, whyever not?"

"They call me names. They say my Daddy's a drunk and my Mama's a tart. What's a tart, Auntie Sairy?"

"Don't you worry about it," I told her. "God judges a person on her own heart, not by what her mama and daddy do. Sometimes people tear other people down in order to raise themselves up higher." I gave her some newspapers and set her to cutting out paper dolls as I'd taught her to, in a chain, hands and feet linked one to the other like Siamese twins. Then she made paper chains to wear as necklaces: one for me, one for her, and one for Holly.

"Aren't you worried about Joleen?" I asked Cate later. "She says she doesn't have any friends. The other kids are making fun of her. When a child doesn't get along at school, she needs her family more than ever. Believe me, Cate, I know."

"Well, what do you expect when her daddy's running around like a dirty dog after a bitch in heat?" she said. "Oh, don't give me that look. You're not going to hell just because you hear a cuss word. We were fine before he started up with you-know-who."

"But Cate, that child needs a proper family. She's raising herself all anyhow. It started long before Gilly's – wandering." I wasn't sure how to allude to it without fanning the flames of Cate's wrath.

"Whose fault is that?" Cate said. "She spends more time here than she does at home."

"And we love to have her," I said hastily, not wanting Cate to keep her away. "She's a good girl."

"You spoil her."

"Now, we don't spoil her," I protested, though actually I realized we did. We closed around Joleen like a fluffy blanket, trying to smother away the traces her parents' hostility left in her heart.

"Don't you set yourself up as a better mother than me, Sairy," Cate warned me. "Joleen is my daughter and don't you forget it. You've got no right to criticize her parents. No wonder she thinks she can sass me when you folks make it clear you think I'm a no-good mother to that child."

"Cate, you know we'd never do that," I said. "We would never countenance Joleen being disrespectful to her mama."

"The way you stuff her full of cookies, she'll be as fat as a pig, too. That's no way for a girl to be popular."

"But she's thin," I protested. "That girl is thin as a rail."

"What are you saying, I don't feed her?" I sighed. Cate seemed determined to take offense at whatever I said, so I let the matter drop.

As the weeks went by, Cate became more and more irritable. She'd bring Joleen by and sit at the kitchen table, brooding.

"Men are scum," she'd say.

"Joleen, honey, why don't you run over to Momma's house and see if she's got any cookies for you?" I shooed her away.

"Don't bad-mouth her daddy in front of her," I scolded Cate. "You pull yourself together. All this fretting isn't going to do you a lick of good. You could use a nice cup of tea yourself."

"What I need's a drink."

"That isn't going to help either," I said. "Now you just forget about Gilly for an hour or two. You stay here and have supper with us tonight."

"I don't want any supper," she'd say, and stalk out to the porch to smoke, one cigarette following the other like a chain of paper dolls, until she threw the last butt away in disgust and drove off again to God only knows where.

One day, she came wearing sunglasses, which she didn't take off when she came into the house.

"What're you wearing those things for?" I asked. "It's cloudy outside."

"I just like 'em," she said. And occasionally after that, she'd have them on again for a few days, regardless of the weather. It caused Virgil to look grim around the mouth.

"What's wrong?" I'd ask. "I guess if she wanted us to know, she'd tell us," he'd say.

I grieved for Cate. It bothered me that I couldn't do anything to help her. She clung to Gilly like a starving man hugging a piece of rotting garbage, refusing to let go of the thing that was making her sick. In desperation, I suggested a thing I never thought I'd say. "Leave him," I said. "Get a divorce. The scripture says it's okay to divorce someone who commits adultery."

"No way," said Cate. "I'll never give him the satisfaction. He won't toss me aside like an old shoe."

***

I guess you're wondering if that pillow I wove did any good at all. I don't know that what it did was good, but it did work. Gilly stopped seeing the other woman. Not because he joined hands with Cate, like I tried to bring about. Instead, he got the other girl pregnant. Cate drove up to the house late one night, with Joleen trailing after her like a puppy. She twisted her ankle on the gravel, but instead of cursing like she usually did, she just giggled. She smelled like rotting fruit, and wasn't too steady on her feet. Virgil and I'd almost finished getting ready for bed when she tottered up the porch steps and pounded on the door. Virgil took one look at her and decided he'd get Joleen to bed over at Momma's house, so he left us in the front room alone together. Cate flopped down in Virgil's chair like a sack of flour.

"It's over," she said, giggling wildly.

"What's over," I said.

"It's over between Gilly and you-know-who. He knocked her up."

"Knocked her up?"

"Got her *pregnant*, Sairy."

"Oh, no."

"Oh, yes. And I know Gilly. He won't have anything to do with a pregnant old cow. He'll dump her like a hot potato."

"Oh, Cate. He can't abandon his own blood like that."

"Whose side are you on, Sairy?" she frowned. "This is what we've been hoping for."

"I never hoped for this," I said. "I wanted him to come back to you, not make a baby and leave it fatherless. This is so awful, I don't know what to think."

"Well I do," she said. "I'm ecstatic. Where's Joleen? I'm gonna go celebrate."

"You've already done some celebrating," Virgil said, coming back in the front door without Joleen.

"Yeah," she said, glancing up at him from the corners of her eyes, "So, what?"

"You need to go on home," he said. "We'll keep Joleen tonight."

"What if I don't want to go home?"

"You can stay here," I said. "Let me get you some nightclothes."

"Oh Sairy. We aren't little girls any more. We don't have sleepovers."

"You can stay at Momma's," I said. "She's got a spare bed for you any time you need it. I don't think you should leave in the shape you're in. What if you get hurt? Come on, Cate. Spend the night here with us. You can go home to Gilly in the morning."

"Gilly's not home. Not yet. I just know he will be."

"I'm not staying," she insisted.

Virgil pulled Cate to her feet and began guiding her inexorably to the door. "You need to go on home," he said again. "You go on home and go to sleep."

"You two are old sticks in the mud," she said. "I don't know why I bother with you." Then, because Virgil was starting to look offended, she added, "Now, Virgil. You know I wouldn't know what to do without you. You're practically family. I get along with you better than my real family, anyway." Then she reeled, falling against him so he had to grab her to keep her from falling down. She kept leaning on him, and wriggled around so they were standing face to face. She put her hands up to his chest and stared foggily into his eyes. "Say, you're pretty strong," she said, as if she'd never noticed before. "I like a strong man."

They stood there like that for several moments before Virgil stood Cate back up on her teetery shoes, turned her around and set her moving in the direction of the car. "Call me in the morning," I said.

Cate didn't call in the morning; instead, she came by late in the afternoon to take Joleen back home. Joleen was standing at Momma's kitchen table, up to her elbows in flour, helping Momma cut out sugar cookies with animal-shaped cookie cutters. Momma had mixed up some egg whites with food coloring so Joleen could paint the cookies before they went into the oven. Meanwhile, I was fussing with the fire to get the oven up to temperature and waiting for a batch of bread dough to rise. I kept nudging Holly out of the way with my ankle because she'd scamper under my feet to bat at the flour that was drifting down from the table. Virgil was out putting new leathers in the pump.

Cate parked at our house, and when she didn't find anyone home, she hallooed and Virgil waved at her from where the pump was, near the chicken yard halfway between Momma's house and ours. I caught sight of them through the window, standing by the pump and talking. Virgil pointed to Momma's house, but Cate didn't walk over; she stayed talking to Virgil, who, in a few minutes, crouched down and went back to his pump repair. Cate bent over his back, perhaps asking a question about the pump, and then seemed to lose her balance and put her hands on his shoulders to steady herself. It didn't look to me like she needed much help, but she stood there for a time with her hands resting on his shoulders.

I must've been transfixed in front of the window, because Joleen called me back to myself by saying, "What're you looking at?"

"Your Mama's here," I said, turning from the window. "You'd better wash your hands."

"I don't wanna go," Joleen pouted. "I wanna finish painting the cookies."

"Young lady," Momma said, "You go wash your hands right now. There'll be more cookies another day."

I stepped out on the porch to call Cate over, and as I did, she straightened up, took her hands from Virgil's shoulders and started picking her way across the ground.

"Did Gilly come home?" I asked.

"Yeah, he came home."

"You-all feeling better?"

"As better as we ever do," she said.

"You want us to go ahead a keep Joleen tonight?" I asked hopefully.

"Nah. We aren't going anywhere."

"I thought maybe you'd want some time together. You know, make up with each other."

Cate shook a cigarette out of her purse and lit it. "I don't think so," she said, and then hollered "Joleen! Get your tail on out here."

"She's washing up," I said. "Her and Momma's been making cookies."

"Well, she needs to scoot," said Cate. "I've got things to do, myself."

Joleen came out of the house, still looking pouty. "C'mon," Cate said, taking her hand and hustling her impatiently off the porch. "Help me back to the car. These shoes aren't made for walking in dirt."

I watched them wobble back to the car, then went back to get my bread in the oven and help Momma finish the cookies. Later, over supper, Virgil told me Cate had asked him to come over and fix something on her car.

"Can't Gilly do that?" I said.

"I guess not," he said flatly. I couldn't tell if he disapproved of it and was trying not to seem that way, or if he had no feelings about it at all.

"When're you going?"

"I told her I guessed I could find some time tomorrow," he said.

I knew Cate couldn't count on Gilly to do for her, but it rankled that she was asking Virgil to take care of things that were Gilly's responsibility. I guess I was jealous. Cate was so pretty, and I knew I was as homely as an old shoe.

Momma advised me not to take it to heart. "Sairy, you know Virgil's a good man," she said. "He'll do no wrong."

She was right, of course. I had nothing but trust in my Virgil; he'd never done a thing to make me fear for his loyalty. And as for Cate, all her nastiness boiled up from a septic, broken place in her heart. It wasn't the real Cate who flirted with Virgil and ignored Joleen and treated me with sneering contempt. Someone had marched all over her tender being like an invading army and left her a trampled ruin. I didn't like her making much of Virgil, but the way I felt, it was random, nothing personal, almost like she couldn't help it. Her wickedness had a hysterical edge of desperation that made me believe she would bash herself to pieces if I didn't treat her gently. So I prayed for patience and then put it out of my mind.

For a while, Virgil ran into Cate frequently, and she always had something she wanted him to do that involved going over to her place. She'd find him at the hardware store or the feed store, or she'd drive on up to our place and track him down at his work, and ask him to dig out her gutters or fix the heater or some such thing. She was always dressed to the nines, and she always stood close to Virgil and kept reaching out to touch him as if she was charged with static electricity and had to ground it on him so she wouldn't float away. She'd fuss with his collar or run a finger down his shirt, or even brush the slab of hair out of his eye. I didn't notice any particular enthusiasm on Virgil's part. He accepted her overtures stoically, sometimes stepping back a hair when she moved in too close, but mostly ignoring them. He didn't spend extra time at her house. He'd go over and do whatever it was she asked, and come right back home, far as I could tell. I'd ask him if Gilly'd been there and he'd usually say he wasn't.

Virgil acted like all these requests were perfectly ordinary. He never made much of them, or of me when he got home, just kissed my cheek as usual. In bed, I could feel his heart beating comfortably against my back, and I knew our marriage was as immovable as the good earth.

I think Gilly knew that Virgil'd been coming over, and he wasn't too happy about it. In fact, thinking back on it, I suspect Cate made up to Virgil on purpose to get back at him. There was something contrary in her, something that wanted Gilly, but at the same time hated her own want and demanded that she drive him to hurt her. Cate wore her sunglasses more often, and Joleen

145

would comment, matter-of-factly, "Mama and Daddy've been fighting again."

I never asked Cate straight out what was going on. I hinted around and tried to get her to confide in me, but she never would. If I asked her about the sunglasses, she'd say she had weak eyes and the light seemed too bright that day. Or she'd say she thought they made her look like a movie star. Or, if she was in a bad mood, she'd just tell me to mind my own business.

"Virgil," I said to him one day, "Gilly hits Cate, doesn't he?"

"Well, it looks that way," he said. "'Course, *I* never see it." He'd confirmed what I'd suspected, and I added Gilly's brutality to the long list of crimes I kept tally of in my mind.

"Why does she let him do it?" I said. "Why does she pretend it's not happening?"

"Honey, I don't know," said Virgil.

"I knew her back when her daddy was beating on her," I said. "She wasn't wearing sunglasses then and saying nothing was wrong. And plus, why do they even stay together? Seems to me like they hate each other."

"Those two are twisted up like two pieces of twine making a rope," he said. And they were. They hated each other and cursed each other and fought with each other, but they were like mice being charmed by a snake – they were frozen to their fatal spot waiting for an inevitable catastrophe.

And catastrophe came. I was the instrument.

# Chapter 12

## ⤷ Catastrophe ⤶

Joleen was supposed to have come to our house that day. It was a school day, so I walked down to where our gravel road meets the pavement, where the bus drops the kids off, but Joleen wasn't on the bus. I figured she'd gotten on the wrong bus and ended up at home, so I called Cate's house, but no one answered. If Cate had changed her mind about Joleen coming, there was no use in driving over there, but for some reason I did it anyway. I wanted to see Joleen, I guess. Momma'd been teaching her to knit, and had just bought a new pattern they wanted to work on together, and we'd already killed and plucked a chicken for her favorite supper. So I climbed in the car and drove to Cate and Gilly's place. When I arrived, I saw their car in the driveway, so I knew they were both at home.

Cate came to the door looking disheveled, in a housecoat and dirty slippers. Her left eye was a virulent bouquet of red and purple, and her lip was swollen and bleeding. There was a string of little bruises on her neck, too, like dark pearls.

"What're you doing here," she croaked as if it was painful to get the words out.

"I'm here because Joleen was supposed to come over to our place today and she wasn't on the bus," I said.

"So she wasn't on the bus," Cate said. "She's staying home tonight."

"Cate, you're hurt. Let me take you to the hospital."

"I'm fine," she said.

"You're not fine. You look terrible. You need to see a doctor."

At that moment, Gilly appeared behind her. His face was in better shape than Cate's, but there were deep scratches down both cheeks and it was ruddy with anger.

"Get the hell out of here," he said.

I don't mind telling you, I was scared to death. Gilly was a big man, and strong, and rage poured off him like heat from a blazing woodstove. But now that I knew what was going on, that Cate and Gilly were fighting like pit bulls, I wasn't going to leave without seeing if Joleen was safe, so I planted my body in the doorway and said

"I'll leave after I see Joleen."

"You're not seeing her," Cate said. "She's in her room. Who do you think you are coming into our house and demanding to see *our* daughter?" She made to close the door, but I stuck my foot in the doorway to block it.

"Joleen!" I called. "Joleen! It's Auntie Sairy! Is everything okay, honey? Why weren't you on the bus?"

Over Gilly's shoulder, I caught a glimpse of movement in the dark hall. A tear-streaked face peered around the corner. "Auntie Sairy!" Joleen cried.

Gilly turned from the door and lunged for Joleen, who started wailing and ran for her bedroom. I bulldozed my way into the house, pushing Cate out of the way, and ran after them down the hall. Gilly caught Joleen before she reached her room and seized her by the hair. He slammed her against the wall and punched her with enough force to bring down a grown man. She fell to the floor and rolled up in a little ball with her arms over her face, and Gilly started kicking her.

I don't remember everything that happened after that. I know I pulled out a hefty handful of Gilly's hair. I remember clinging to his back like a cowboy on a bull as he bellowed and smashed his back, with me on it, against the wall over and over, trying to shake me loose. I remember running to the kitchen and grabbing the cast iron frying pan off the stove. I might've gotten in a few whacks with it before I heard the siren of a police car coming up the road. One of the neighbors had called the police because I'd been screaming like a banshee the whole time.

Gilly didn't stay around to talk to the police. As soon as he realized they were coming, he took off out the back door. The police found me, Cate and Joleen, all looking pretty battered. They wanted to know what in the Sam Hill the ruckus was all about. In those days, we didn't call it domestic violence when a husband and wife got into a fight, and we didn't put people in jail for it. The police just wanted us to hush up and stop disturbing the neighbors.

I started shouting about Gilly kicking Joleen, but Cate lied and said Joleen'd had an accident at school, and I'd pushed my way into the house, was interfering in their family business, would the police please make me go away. The noise was my fault, she said; I'd riled up her husband and caused the whole thing. So the police told me to go on home if I didn't want to get in trouble, and hustled me out the door.

"I'm not leaving without Joleen," I said, and burst into tears. "That was no accident. Gilly punched her."

"You shut your lying mouth," Cate shouted, and then to the police, "Get her out of here."

"Lady, either you leave now or you leave in a squad car," they said.

What could I do? Joleen wasn't mine. Before I drove home, though, I sat in the car and sobbed for a while, hoping maybe Cate would relent and let Joleen come home with me. I'd never been in a fight in my whole life. My ribs hurt, and my face hurt...I hurt all over. Worse, though, was the thought that Joleen was still in that house and I couldn't get to her.

I was furious at Cate. How could she let Gilly do that to her own daughter? How could she take his side? Every time I thought about little Joleen rolled up in a ball on the floor and Gilly whacking away at her with his boot, I wanted to tear his head off. It was a good thing Virgil'd never been a hunter. If we'd had a gun in the car, I might've shot Gilly dead that very night.

I waited so long the police came out to the car and told me I was asking for trouble, and when they looked again, I'd better be gone. So I mopped the mess off my face with my skirt and drove away. When I finally got home and Virgil saw the shape I was in, his eyes got squinty and his face reddened.

"What's this?" he said. "What happened to you?"

I started crying again. "Gilly," I said. "Gilly. I went over to get Joleen, and – and he wouldn't let her come to the door. He chased her into the hall and started whomping on her. So I tried to stop him."

I'd never seen Virgil so mad. "Gilly did this to you? Gilly hit *my wife*? We'll see about this. Get out of the car."

He opened the door and scooped me out of the seat. His hands were shaking. He set me down and made to get in himself, but I clung to his arm with both hands and started pulling, trying to get him away and back to the house.

"Don't go," I begged him. I saw the way his thoughts were running. He was ready to drive over to Gilly's house and beat him to a pulp. "If I'd've left when he told me to, he wouldn't've hit me," I said.

"Let go of my arm, Sairy. I'm not letting any man do this to my wife," he said.

"It's my fault," I insisted. "I – I jumped on him when he punched Joleen. I pulled out his hair. I tried to hit him with the frying pan."

"That's no reason to hit a woman."

"Please don't go, Virgil. Please. I'm afraid of what might happen." Virgil looked unconvinced, but he stopped trying to shake me off his arm.

"Please. Please," I begged. "Please. For my sake, don't do anything, Virgil. I can't live without you. Please just let it be."

I don't think Virgil was happy about it. In his mind, it wasn't right for a man to stand by while someone beat up his wife. But, for my sake, because I begged him, he gave in to me.

"Let's get you into the house," he said. He closed the car door.

"Get the keys," I said. So he did, and gave them to me because I pleaded he would. He helped me into the house, then, and tended my hurts as gently as a mother. Although I was as angry as he, I wanted to make sure he'd go nowhere near Gilly that night, or for a long time. Virgil wasn't a piece-of-nothing woman Gilly could bang up against the wall and toss out of the house. I was afraid he'd meet Virgil at the door with a gun. So, even though I wanted to take Gilly apart with a butcher knife, I begged Virgil not to confront him. Instead, I made my own plan.

\*\*\*

The next morning, I got up before the sun rose, while Virgil was still snoring away under the piece quilt Momma'd given us for Christmas a few years earlier. I took my loom from its place on the shelf over the bar Virgil'd put up on the wall to hang clothes on. I cut the web off of it – a piece I'd been weaving for part of a new tablecloth for Momma. And I sat down to weave something for Gilly.

It was the first time, and the last, I ever purposely wove with hatred in my heart. I let it swell like a bloody tide as I strung the warps and wound the shuttle. The picture of Gilly grabbing Joleen by the hair, punching and kicking her, replayed over and over again in my mind. I made no effort to turn my thoughts elsewhere. I bathed in anger. I immersed myself in hatred. I burned with a desire for vengeance.

You might've thought such hatred would make my fingers clumsy, but not so. They flew to their work quick as little sparks popping from the fire. Before Virgil arose, I'd strung the loom and woven a whole inch of the web.

When he woke up, I abandoned the work, pretending it was an ordinary piece, nothing important, and went into the kitchen to make him breakfast. After serving him, I sat across his lap for a minute and cuddled up against his chest.

"Thank you for staying with me last night, Virgil."

"Um," he said, and I knew he was still uneasy about not taking Gilly to task.

There must've been something peculiar in my manner, too, because he looked long at me before asking, "Anything wrong?"

"Not a thing," I answered.

"You feeling all right this morning? Not too sore? You look pretty banged up. You might want to take it easy for a couple days."

My ribs stabbed me every time I breathed in. My neck felt like a wrung chicken. My head was bruised and tender where Gilly'd banged it into the wall.

"I'm fine," I said. "I feel just fine."

"You've got a black eye," he said.

"It doesn't hurt all that much."

"Fire's not going."

"It will be."

And it would, I swore to myself. I'd light a fire that'd burn Gilly up like a piece of tissue paper. I saw him burning every time I sat down to work on the loom. Burn, I thought. And after you die, burn some more.

The piece took me only five days to complete. I wove it of cotton warps and good, stiff wool so it'd be warm. It was made from woodland colors: mossy green with brown threads. When I looked at it, though, I saw it ringed with a faint, red smudge. My anger was pouring off it in a hot flood.

I couldn't just walk over and hand the scarf to Gilly. Nobody'd believe I wanted to give him a gift, not even Gilly. He'd probably think there was a black widow spider wrapped up inside, and for sure he'd never wear it. So I took it over to Cate's house and hid it in his drawer. I didn't figure anyone over there would notice it was new or care where it came from.

I was nervous about facing Cate. I feared she wouldn't even let me in the house after what she said about me that night. But somehow, I'd just have to bring her around. I put on one of Virgil's jackets, rolled up the scarf and put it in the pocket to hide it.

Cate answered my knock, and came to the door looking defensive.

"How you doing?" I asked cautiously.

"Fine," she said.

"Where's Joleen?"

"She's at school. It's a school day."

"Is she okay?"

"Of course she's okay. She got a spanking. Is she supposed to stay home from school for a week because she had a spanking?"

"Cate, that wasn't a spanking. I saw Gilly kick that child."

"Sairy, I'm warning you. You stay out of our business. Just because I've known you since I was a girl doesn't mean you have a right to interfere when Joleen's father disciplines her."

"Discipline. You ought to know better," I said. "Your own father used to beat you up."

"Yes, my own father used to beat me up, and I lived to tell the tale. Joleen needs to mind her father. I'm not saying Gilly doesn't go a little too far sometimes, but she brings it on herself."

"That is just ridiculous. How did she bring all that on herself the other night?" I said, suddenly angry.

"She should've stayed in her room and kept quiet like her father told her. She had no business running around the house hollering at the door."

"She wasn't hollering. She said 'hello' to me."

"Well, you didn't have any business calling to her. In fact, you didn't have any business coming over in the first place."

"That's just about the sorriest excuse I've ever heard for beating a child. What about when he beats *you*? Do you bring it on yourself, too?"

"What're you talking about?"

"I'm talking about the bruises you hide behind those sunglasses. I'm talking about all that mess on your face and neck the other night. Why, your eye is still yellow and black. Are you saying Gilly didn't give you that?"

Cate turned away. "What did you come here for? To nose around in other peoples' business causing trouble again? Or did you have an actual reason?"

"I think I dropped Momma's pin the other night," I said.

"I haven't seen any pin."

"Well, I'm pretty sure it fell off my dress when Gilly was...it fell off back in the hall there. Maybe it got kicked into a corner somewhere. Can I look for it?"

"I guess."

I came into the house. "Cate, honey, let's not argue. Let's sit down together and have some tea. You look tired."

Actually, Cate looked more used up than tired. Her skin was desiccated and fragile-looking as if someone had taken a straw and sucked all the water right out of her. Her hair, which she usually took such pains to keep nice, was frizzy and ragged. I shepherded her into the living room and went to put the kettle on. Then, while I was waiting for it to boil, I went back to Cate and Gilly's room, took the rolled-up scarf out of my pocket, folded it and placed it in one of Gilly's drawers. There weren't a lot of clothes in the dresser. Most of them were flung willy-nilly around the room, hanging on the backs of chairs and wadded up on the floor. His top drawer had a pile of wool socks in it, and I put the scarf on top of those where he'd be sure to find it.

Then, I went to the kitchen to make me and Cate some tea. I had to wash a couple of mugs and dig through a cupboard all filmed over with spilled rice and flour to find a box of tea bags. When I came back to the living room with the mugs in my hand, Cate was slumped on the couch with her head propped up on one hand.

Did I feel like a traitor? No. I felt like a deliverer, a sword of righteousness.

"Cate," I said. "What's wrong, honey? Isn't there something I can do to help? I just hate to see you like this."

"Oh, Sairy. I'm not cut out to be a wife and mother." She took the tea and sipped without picking her head up off her hand.

"You are too. It isn't you that's the problem."

"You don't know. You don't understand. I just get so *angry* sometimes. I feel cheated. Why does everyone else have it so easy and I have it so hard? Why doesn't he love me? Why doesn't anyone love me?"

"We love you," I said. "Me and Virgil and Momma all love you."

"It's not the same. It's not what I need. I need to be the most important thing in someone's life. I need someone to feel like 'I'd do anything for her. I'd give up anything. I'd die for her.' Instead I get 'you're a pretty hot number, but I'm going back to my wife'. I get 'I'm sick of hearing you bitch about what a slob I am. I'm going out and find me a woman who appreciates me.' How come they never appreciate *me*? Why is it always me that has to do all the appreciating?"

By now, the tears were running down her cheeks. I just sat on the couch pressing one of her hands in both of mine, helpless. I didn't know what to say. Why *did* she always wind up with men who didn't appreciate her? You'd think someone so bright and pretty would have the pick of the litter. You'd think it'd be the people like me, the plain, ordinary ones, who'd get dumped and slapped around.

"Poor Catie," I said. "There, there, now. It's going to be all right, honey. It'll get better; you'll see."

I thought about that scarf sitting in Gilly's top drawer, and I felt triumph rising in me like boiling water. I didn't know how it'd happen, but I knew he was about to get his come-uppance.

*** 

It was a hunting accident.

Gilly hadn't worn the scarf right away. But the snow came early that year. When hunting season rolled around, he'd gone through that drawer looking for something to keep warm out in the woods and he'd run across the scarf. He'd wrapped it around his neck, not knowing it'd turn on him like a hungry Anaconda, and stumped out into the woods with a couple of his friends. They were drinking, like always. They shot up some trees and a couple of road signs. Then, as they were carousing around the fire after nightfall, one of them shot Gilly. Didn't see him in the dark, he swore. Saw him sitting at the campfire, plain as day, and thought he heard an animal creeping through the woods. Didn't see how someone as drunk as Gilly, who could hardly stand up, could've made the stealthy half-noises he heard before he shot.

I wasn't surprised in the least. I could see in my mind's eye the blanket of invisibility that scarf had wrapped around him as he stumbled through the woods, looking for a place to do his business, I imagine. I could see the roaring, singing, large-as-life image it projected into their midst as they drank and hollered around the fire. They wouldn't have seen him if it'd been broad daylight and he was standing five feet away, waving and calling their names. His demise was as inevitable as sunrise, made certain the minute he wound that scarf around his sorry neck.

By the time they dragged him out of the woods, he was already dead. They threw him in the back of his own pickup and drove him to the hospital, but when they loaded him on a stretcher and carried him into the emergency room, he was cold and blue and stiff as an icicle. We heard the story from one of Cate's neighbors who called to ask if we'd come take care of Joleen...Cate'd left her home alone when she went down to the hospital.

I was glad it'd been Virgil who took the call. Virgil was a good man, and he was innocent of any crime toward Gilly. He could sound shocked and concerned as he asked what on earth happened, inquired after Cate and promised we'd be right over to get Joleen. Myself, I felt no abatement of the rage that'd led me to put that poisonous scarf in Gilly's drawer. All that happened was that it went from hot to Arctic cold. My rage was as cold as Gilly's body. I knew he was dead before Virgil even put down the phone.

And here's what I thought about it: 'It's about time.'

That's when I knew there was evil lurking in my heart. Oh, I'd been raised to be a nice, Christian woman. I didn't gossip, nor defy my husband's authority. I didn't complain about what the Lord put in front of me. I did as I was taught. But under all that, wickedness flowed like a stinking tide. I could hate a man, and bring about his death without losing a minute of sleep over it. In

157

fact, I could rejoice about it and think the world was well rid of him.

I met my own demon that day. You'd have thought it'd scare me, or that I'd shrink from it in revulsion, but that didn't happen. I stared it down, unblinking, and nodded my head as if to say, "I know you. You're part of me. Come right on in and make yourself at home."

\*\*\*

Virgil and Momma and I went to the funeral, of course. I didn't want to let Joleen go, and Cate and I argued bitterly about it.

"She ought to go to her own father's funeral," Cate said.

"She doesn't need to be there," I insisted. "She's young. It's bad enough she's lost her father. Don't make her go and look at his dead body. It's morbid."

Privately, I wanted to protect Joleen. Just in case she was more relieved than sorry that Gilly was gone, as I was.

"You're wrong," Cate said. "She needs to say goodbye to him. He's her Daddy."

But I had my way. Joleen didn't go; she stayed with one of the ladies from church while we-all went to pay our respects. I think Cate was so lost she couldn't even keep her mind on arguing.

Cate carried on through the whole funeral as if it'd been her child she lost rather than a two-timing husband. Rivers of tears and mucus ran down her face. She could hardly sit up, the sobs were wracking her body so hard.

Virgil and Momma and I sat right next to her, propping her up, mopping her face, and shielding her from everyone else's view. We were a little island of folks on one side of the church, while all Gilly's family and friends sat on the other as if they couldn't stand to be near her. As if they were blaming her for Gilly's drunken accident in the woods.

I was amazed at how many people turned out for Gilly. When he was alive, you couldn't find a sober person in town that had a good word to say about him. Now that he was dead, they sat in somber reverence, dabbing their eyes and nodding at the preacher's comforting words like the center of the universe had just been ripped away and left us all floating in the dark with no gravity, but it was okay because Jesus had called this fine young man home to a better place.

Gilly was good and dead, all right. If he hadn't been, he would've sat up in his coffin and cursed them all out for fools, starting with the preacher. There's little good I can say about Gilly, but he wasn't a hypocrite. He wouldn't have sat through a sermon for his own Mama, much less for himself. If he'd known what was going on, he probably would've asked everyone at that funeral what in the Sam Hill they thought they were doing, reading scripture over him when all he wanted was a drink and a dance, thank you.

When the preacher had finished telling us all what a great loss we'd suffered in seeing the back of Gilly, we filed past the body, Momma, me and Virgil first in line after Cate. Gilly looked unnatural. His face was calm, with all the ruddiness washed out of his complexion. I never saw him look peaceful before, never saw him when he wasn't frowning or hollering. Pale, diaphanous eyelids covered his close-set eyes, and his blunt-fingered hands were clasped reverently over his breast like carven ivory. He looked like a statue. He was wearing an ill-fitting suit, the one he'd gotten married in which he'd never worn since.

Cate threw herself over the open casket wailing "Gilly, Gilly, my darling husband!" Momma gently pried her off and led her back to her pew. I just stood and stared at Gilly until Virgil nudged me along with a firm hand in the small of my back. I wore

159

a black armband, but perversely, I'd put on a dress covered with lavender flowers, my favorite church dress. It was my secret Hallelujah, my badge of evil.

At the cemetery, after they lowered Gilly into the ground, we each took a handful of dirt and threw it over the coffin.

"This's the end," I told Gilly silently as I tossed the dirt at the spot where I thought his face might be. "You'll never hurt Cate and Joleen again."

I was wrong about so many things. That was only one of them.

# Chapter 13

# The Aftermath

A few weeks after Gilly's death, we moved Cate back into Momma's place. She'd run out of money and had nowhere else to go. Joleen came to our house from school one day, complaining she was hungry.

"Didn't you have lunch, honey?" Momma asked.

Joleen shook her head. "Mama didn't make me any," she said.

"Well, what about breakfast? Did you have your breakfast?"

"Mama hasn't been shopping," she said. "A man came to the door asking for money. He said if we didn't give it to him, he'd kick us out. Mama gave him all the grocery money, but it wasn't enough. He came back the next day and Mama hid in the bedroom while I answered the door."

We left Joleen with Momma, piled into the car and went to collect Cate. She came to the door in an old housecoat of Gilly's, sagging at the hem and speckled with cigarette burns.

"Joleen says you're out of money," I said.

"That's right," Cate replied.

"Didn't Gilly leave you any?"

"Only what was in his wallet. I gave that to the landlord two days ago. He said he'll be back with the sheriff to throw us out."

"Let's get your things and get out of here," Virgil said. "You're moving in with Momma where we can look after the two of you."

We couldn't take much, but there wasn't much in the house worth taking: a few battered pieces of furniture and Cate and Joleen's clothes. We left the dirty dishes in the sink, the furniture and all of Gilly's old things, stuffing Cate and Joleen's clothes, mostly unlaundered, into bags, which we stacked in the trunk and back seat of the car. Cate showed no interest in what we were packing until we came from her bedroom carrying the last of the bags.

"Gilly's hunting cap," she said.

Virgil saw I was about to argue, and put his hand on my arm. He returned to the bedroom wordlessly and came out with a sweat-stained, woolen hunting cap in his hand.

"This it?"

"Yes." Cate grabbed the hat and clutched it to chest like a life preserver. Then, she let Virgil lead her out of the house and put her in the car.

It made me sad to leave the house like that, squalid with the residue of Cate and Gilly's life. Still, I thought, she'd be better out of the place. Gilly's presence permeated it like a noisome stench. At home, where everything was clean and cozy, she could sweep the muck out of her mind and find some peace.

At first, we put Cate and Joleen together in Danny's and my old room upstairs at Momma's house. But Cate didn't sleep much. She sat up all night with the lights on, rocking back and forth on the bed, crooning to Gilly's old hunting cap until Momma said it'd be best to move Joleen over with Virgil and me 'til Cate got back on her feet. So a couple of days later, we made Joleen a little bed pallet in our living room, and there she stayed, waiting for Cate to come to her senses. It was a long wait.

I hoped that Cate would forget Gilly, or at least, as time went on, see that she was better off without him. Instead, she gathered up the frayed threads of their past and wove them into a bizarre fantasy of tenderness and love that never existed.

"I just can't fathom how I'm going to get along without him," she sighed. "I feel like I'm trying to live with half my body cut off."

Joleen was sitting right there at the table with us and I didn't want to speak ill of her father in front of her, so I just nodded. Later, though, when Cate and I were alone, I brought it up again.

"I can't believe you'd say a thing like that," I told her. "Gilly was pure poison to you. You were never happy one minute with him."

"That's not true," she said, tensing up so the wrinkles which had started creeping in around her mouth deepened to hard creases. "You never understood Gilly and me."

"I know he was your husband, and for that, you had to respect him," I said. "But I never understood why you let him beat up on Joleen. And I think I understood Gilly just fine. He was a man with a bad streak. He was a bad husband and a bad father."

"Shut up," she said. "Just shut up. If you and your precious Virgil hadn't always been throwing things in our face, trying to come between us and our own daughter, maybe he wouldn't have been that way."

"Cate, you're talking crazy. Gilly was a wild boy from the start. He left you sitting in the hall at your own wedding. He committed adultery with another woman, and then left her cold when he got her pregnant. Virgil and I didn't make him that way. He was that way before he even met you."

"I loved him!" she cried. "I loved him! I don't care what you say. He was my husband and I wish I'd died with him."

"What about Joleen?" I said. "What about your sweet, precious child? What would become of her if she lost both her mama and her daddy?"

"She's got you and Virgil. She loves you better than me anyway. You've seen to that. She'd do fine."

"Now Cate, you know Virgil and I don't want to steal Joleen's love away from you. You know she'll always love you best. You just aren't thinking straight. Can't you see how much better off you are without Gilly all the time making you miserable with his cheating and beating?"

"Gilly loved me," she said.

"Well, he sure had a funny way of showing it."

"Oh Sairy." Cate slumped against the wall and started to pick at her fingernails. "Can't you see how empty I am? I feel all hollow inside. Every morning I wake up and wonder 'what's the use of even getting out of bed today'. I've got no man. Nobody to be pretty for. Nobody to live for."

"Cate," I said, hoping I wasn't starting another argument, "You can get over this. Remember that married man you were with over in the city? Remember what it was like when you broke up with him? You got along, didn't you? You had a hard time for a while, but you survived. You're still young. You'll find another man, a better man."

She looked at me dully. The pupils in her eyes were dilated so her eyes looked almost black.

"I slit my wrists, is what happened," she said.

"What?"

"I cut myself up. I tried to kill myself when he dumped me and went back to his wife."

"Cate, that's a sin." The words were out before I had time to think.

"Oh, you and your sin," she said. "I'm hurting bad enough to die and all you can do is talk about your stupid God and his stupid sin."

I put my arms around her but she kept her arms clamped to her sides, rigid as a dead stick.

"I'm sorry, Cate," I said. "I'm sorry. I didn't mean it. Don't get mad at God because of what I say. You know I'm not smart like you."

"I don't know about that, Sairy," she said, pulling back from my embrace and looking at me strangely. "Sometimes I wonder just how smart you really are. I think there's more going on in there than you let on."

I backed away and left her standing in the kitchen, went off by myself to mull over what she'd said. How much did she know, or had she guessed, about that scarf? Up until the day I'd started weaving it, I'd thought I couldn't step across the line of wickedness, that I was too rooted in the Bible to even think of such an unholy thing and too meek to act on it if I did. But when I saw the blood and tears running down Joleen's face, all my years of piety were swept away before a tide of vengeful hatred. I was filled with wrath that knew no restraint. I believed that ridding the world of Gilly was justifiable.

In my heart of hearts, God forgive me, I still believe it.

This wasn't the last conversation we had about Gilly. In fact, it was as if I'd opened the door to all Cate's irrational thoughts, and from that time on they poured from her lips in a relentless flood. She abused herself, and me, and Virgil, and even Joleen, blaming each of us in turn for Gilly's wrongdoing. She spoke of Gilly as a victim, then built him up to be a full-fledged martyr. The world had misshaped him, misunderstood him, then rejected and killed him. You'd have thought she was talking about Jesus, himself.

As time went on, the Gilly of Cate's imagining bore less and less resemblance to the loud, brash, mean-spirited man I remembered. First, Cate's attitude mystified me, and later it disgusted me. I didn't want to hear any more tall tales about Saint

Gilly, so I started ignoring her whenever she began to carry on about him.

Instead of taking solace in Joleen, who followed her around like a puppy, offering to fetch her comb or her sweater or pick up her room, or anything to get her attention, she paid her no mind at all.

"I love you, Mommy." Joleen would say, "Don't be sad." And she'd try to lay her head on Cate's lap.

Cate would stare out the window, then rise abruptly to her feet and flee to Momma's house as if she couldn't bear to hear her daughter's voice.

"Come on over here to your Aunt Sairy," I'd say, and gather her into my arms.

"Why does Mama hate me?" she asked.

"Your Mama doesn't hate you," I said. But I wondered if she did. Maybe Cate sensed without knowing that the night Gilly beat up on Joleen was the night his death had been set in motion as inevitably as dark follows sunset. I wondered if she figured it was Joleen's fault, that if Joleen hadn't been there and Gilly hadn't beat her up, he'd never have died.

*\*\**

Christmas came not too long after Gilly died. Since Virgil'd gotten the farm going strong, we had a little more money than we used to when I was a girl, but we didn't change the way we celebrated on account of that. The old ways were a joy to us. Virgil cut down a pine tree and we set it up right near Joleen's bed pallet. She could pretend she was sleeping in a tree house with the resinous perfume of pine all hovering around her pillow.

Joleen strung popcorn and cut out tin foil ornaments to decorate the tree just as Danny I used to do. Only now, Virgil delighted Joleen by pretending to "help" with bumbling incompetence – he couldn't thread the needle, he complained, and then he couldn't get it through the popcorn without breaking the kernels all to pieces. So Joleen bossed him around while he meekly said "Yes, ma'am" and "No, ma'am" and cut paper doll strings out of tinfoil that didn't join the way they were supposed to. Pretty soon, Joleen was shrieking with laughter and the two of them were throwing popcorn at each other.

"You two are worse than a couple of kids," Momma said. "When you're done making a pigsty out of this kitchen, you can get the broom and sweep every bit of this popcorn off the floor."

"Yes, ma'am," Virgil said.

Cate didn't join in their hilarity, but refused both needle and scissors. Instead, she rocked listlessly in Momma's chair with a Christmas cookie crumbling in her hand. Before the tree was even decorated, she went back to her room to huddle alone on the bed with Gilly's hat.

I'd sewed Virgil a shirt, and Joleen a dress from the same fabric. When they ripped open the packages and found their matching outfits, they put them on and waltzed around the kitchen together while we all sang Christmas carols. Then Joleen climbed into my lap and rested her head against my heart while Virgil read us the Christmas story from the book of Luke. I'd given Momma and Cate things I'd sewn as well, Momma an apron and Cate a skirt. Joleen gave everyone jam made from wild blackberries that Momma'd showed her how to cook.

Cate gave nothing, even to Joleen.

"I don't see why we have to have all this fuss," she complained to me. "We've got nothing to celebrate."

"There's plenty to celebrate," I said. "You've got a snug home and a loving family. Besides, there's Joleen to think about. Don't you want her to have a happy Christmas?"

"Happy, unhappy. What difference does it make? Life is unhappy. She might as well get used to it. Anyway, you're encouraging her to forget her father."

"She won't forget him," I said.

How *could* she, is what I didn't say.

I got used to pretending Cate didn't mean all she said. I wanted everything to be good, or at least better than it was before. I wanted her to think, as I did, that Gilly was gone and best forgotten. I wanted her to love Joleen. I wanted her to be a different person than she was.  I wanted it so badly that I pretended it was so.

Momma did the same, or so it seemed to me, but maybe she just couldn't think of anything else to do.

"Now stop moping," she'd tell Cate, and bustle around the house, ordering her to pick this up or sweep that up, as if keeping her busy would lift her up out of the well she seemed to have fallen down into. Only Virgil took her seriously. He watched her closely, shaking his head and frowning over her declarations that she'd be better off dead.

When I look back, I realize I should've seen it was only a matter of time before she was. The strange thing was how long she waited. I could've understood her killing herself in a frenzy of grief right at the first. But instead, she waited for months and months, tormenting herself, and all of us, with her apathy and bitterness.

She took to walking through the woods, in all kinds of weather. She went out without a jacket in her flimsy shoes, coming back after dark, soaked through, muddy and shivering.

"You'll catch your death," Momma scolded.

"Good," she'd reply.

"You have to let him go. You have to go on living for Joleen's sake."

"I can't. I don't want to."

"You're not doing yourself any good this way. I know it's hard, child. I'm a widow, too. But I had to get by for Sairy and

Danny's sake, so I did. You'll feel differently after a while. You'll get better."

"I don't want to," Cate said.

Momma didn't understand, and neither did I. I never knew a person could clutch onto pain the same way I clutch onto happiness.

\*\*\*

When she finally did it, she made sure it was Joleen who'd find her. Joleen had formed the habit of bringing her a cup of tea while she lingered in bed in the mornings. She'd bring it upstairs right before she walked down to catch the school bus and kiss her goodbye. Then, one morning, Joleen brought the tea and found her mother sleeping, as she thought. She put the tea down on the nightstand and leaned over to give her a kiss.

A moment later, she came tumbling down the stairs, screaming, "Gamma, Auntie Sairy! There's something wrong with Mama," and burst into tears.

Momma and I raced upstairs and found Cate cold in the bed, eyes open and staring.

I was stunned. But also, I was furious at Cate for killing herself and letting Joleen find her. I was angry that she'd stayed with Gilly in the first place, and angry that she'd lied to herself about what kind of man he was. And I was mad that she'd pushed us away as if our love meant nothing. As if it couldn't compare with what she got from her no-good husband.

As I stood beside Momma and stared at Cate lying in Danny's old bed, pale and stiff as a porcelain doll, I started to know my own jealous heart. Because somewhere in my mind this thought was lurking: "Joleen's better off without you."

I wanted to protect Joleen. I thought I'd wanted to protect Cate. But I'd given up on her somewhere along the way. She was wild, and stubborn, and cold to Joleen. Her whole being was obsessed with Gilly, Gilly, Gilly. She had no time or love left over for us. For me.

Not once did I think blame on myself for starting the whole thing, for defying God's will and weaving a layette that brought a child into the world whose parents didn't want her. The germ of evil is subtle and easy to justify. Only later, when it's too late to rip the web up and start again, can you see the implications of what you've done. I can see it now. But here's the sin: even knowing what I know, I wouldn't change it. I wouldn't unmake Joleen for anyone's sake, not Cate's, not Virgil's, and certainly not Gilly's.

"Go get Virgil," Momma said.

We had to have the police up, of course. They had to call the coroner, and he had to declare Cate's death a suicide. She'd left an empty sleeping-pill bottle on the bedside table, but nothing else, no note, no apology, not a word to any of us. Not even a good-bye to her own daughter.

We had her body cremated, and scattered the ashes under the birch trees where she and I used to play, where, in the late springtime, a seasonal creek trickles down through the draw into the pond. We thought she'd get comfort from the sweet chuckling of the water and the transparent gold of leaves turning in the fall.

I still walk there sometimes, although the heavy underbrush claws at my legs and conceals the ground, making it hard to tell exactly where we put her. The birches we played beneath are gone, fallen and rotting, or harvested for firewood, and replaced by a new generation of saplings all sprung up in different spots. Only the rocks are still there.

There's one in particular, a dome-shaped chunk of granite half buried in the ground that each of us used to stand on while the other tried to push her off. Or, we'd sit our dolls with their backs to the rock and set a tea party of mud cookies and twig silverware in front of them. I imagine that was a happy time for Cate, as it was for me, perhaps one of the few happy times she ever had.

When we lost Cate, Joleen became my daughter in all but name. I had a moment of fear that her grandmother, Gilly's Ma, would try to take her, but Gilly's people weren't interested in the child. They even called her paternity into question, as if it'd been Cate, rather than Gilly, who philandered. I overheard Gilly's mother in the grocery store one day, spewing poisonous gossip to one of her friends.

"She was a tart shined up with town polish," she said, "and she ran my son into his grave."

Well, I'd never been one to argue with people before Gilly's death, and surely not in public with a person who was practically a stranger. But her nasty remark lit a spark of rebellion in me that burned up my former timidity and fear of rudeness. I guess a murderer doesn't worry much about what people think. I marched right up, planted myself at her elbow and stared her straight in the face.

"I suppose it was Cate's fault Gilly got liquored up and got himself shot," I said.

"Who are *you*?" she said, moving away from me as if I had cooties wandering around on my forehead.

"I'm Sairy Talbert," I said. "And I was a friend of your son's wife. The wife who sat at home while he ran around town getting drunk and fooling around with other women."

"You're intruding on a *private* conversation, Sairy Talbert," she said. "You mind your own business."

"I'll mind my own business when you stop spreading hateful lies about my friend," I said.

"I never," she said to her friend. "Some people are bold as brass."

She took the other lady by the arm and left the store with an air of outraged dignity. I guess she didn't stop talking, because I heard gossip about it all over town. She busied herself re-making Gilly as Cate's wronged husband.

"I want to go over to her house and give her a piece of my mind," I told Momma.

"Leave it alone," she advised. "No good can come of interfering. She's lost her son. It's a hard thing to lose your son." She looked sad, and I realized she felt sorry for Gilly's mother as I never could. They had something in common I couldn't share in.

Meanwhile, poor, little Joleen was coming apart at the seams. She had nightmares about corpses under the bed and in the closet. She wouldn't go anywhere alone in the dark, even into the next room.

"Why'd Mama die?" she asked.

"I don't know," I lied.

"Tell her the truth," Virgil said. "Your Mama was unhappy. She took her own life."

"Birdie told me Mama's going to hell."

"Who's Birdie?"

"A girl at school."

"Well, Birdie doesn't know. Hell is between your Mama and God. Birdie has nothing to say about it."

"Birdie says people who kill themselves are going to hell. She says Mama was a bad woman. Is that true?"

"No," Virgil said. "Your mama wasn't a bad woman. She was an unhappy woman. That isn't the same thing."

"What about Daddy? Was he a bad man?"

"YES," I wanted to scream, but I kept quiet.

"Good and bad isn't for us to judge," Virgil said. "Everyone does bad things sometimes."

"Then why does everyone say Mama was bad?"

"Because that's the way people are. They always see the bad in other people better than they see their own bad."

"I wish Mama hadn't killed herself."

"Me, too, honey."

"Are you going to die?"

"Some day I will. Not for a long time, though."

"What'll happen to me after you die? And Auntie Sairy? And Gamma?"

"You'll be all right. By then, you'll have a family of your own. You'll be an old lady, just like your Auntie Sairy."

"I'm not old," I said.

Virgil patted my hip. "You're older than Joleen."

"Don't you worry about people dying," I told her. "You worry about getting good grades. We aren't going to die."

I began to notice Joleen fussing over Holly, who by now was a fat, sedentary old tabby that lay around shedding on Virgil's favorite chair.

"You need exercise," she'd tell Holly, chasing her outside. "You're gonna get a heart attack."

"Honey, you leave that cat alone," I said. "She's just fine where she is."

"In health class, they told us we have to exercise. We have to exercise every day so we don't die of a heart attack."

"Cats are different," I said. "They need lots of sleep. Come set the table for me. It's getting on toward supper time."

We did everything we could for Joleen, but we couldn't stop her from fretting. We couldn't stop her from wondering why, in one short year, she'd lost both her father and her mother. We couldn't keep her from feeling vulnerable, nor from thinking about death more than a child ever should.

We also couldn't stop her from getting teased by the other kids at school. They taunted her so mercilessly about her father the drunk and her mother the floozy that she turned from the bright, happy child we knew before into a timid wallflower. She walked around with a permanent hunched-over look as if to ward off the cruelty she expected would fall on her at any moment like a dead branch blown out of a tree.

# Chapter 14

# Joleen, Part 2

They say that time's a healer. Now that I had everything I ever wanted: Momma, Virgil and Joleen all wound around me like a ball of wool, you'd think I'd walk in blessedness. It didn't happen that way. Oh, my life wasn't a string of catastrophes. It was peaceable and calm, as usual. We farmed, we canned, we gardened and baked. I wove. But with Cate gone, it was like the center of my life had been dislodged. I had trouble fixing my feet on the ground. I'd catch myself saying to Joleen, "You better ask your Mama about that," or to Virgil, "Tell Cate I need help with the milking this morning." Her presence haunted the place, and I felt like she was just temporarily out of sight, around a corner or in another room instead of gone for good.

She infiltrated my weaving, too. As I sat down to the loom, I'd see her wandering the draw in her flimsy shoes, water dripping down her neck and damp leaves clustered in her hair. Or, I'd hear her squeaky, out-of-tune voice floating on the breeze from Momma's house, humming along with the radio some "he done me wrong" song. Then, I'd look down at the web and realize she was lurking there like a dusty film smeared over the clear colors of the weft. I'd have to rip it all out, roll the loom up and put it back on the shelf.

I didn't know how to do for Joleen, either. We took her to church, of course. We shielded her from the gossip-mongers there. Whenever someone tried to pry out information or preach at her under the guise of "sympathy", Momma'd zoom in and send them packing.

"You poor child," Mrs. So-and-So would say, "I guess you miss your Mama something terrible. That terrible way she died...what was it, sleeping pills?"

Or "I imagine you must worry about your Mama and Daddy, hon, the way they went. It's a wicked world we live in, and only the pure in heart will see God."

Momma had a nose for it. She'd smell dung under the honey from halfway across the church, sweep up behind Joleen and plant a hand on each shoulder. "That's no fit way to speak to a child," she'd say. "Think shame to yourself. 'If any think they are religious and do not bridle their tongues, but deceive their hearts, their religion is worthless.'"

"Now, I didn't mean any harm."

And Momma would guide Joleen back to where I was standing, listening to Virgil talk crops and animals with one of the neighbors.

When Joleen got to high school, she started hanging around with girls who smoked and wore short skirts, and boys who grew their hair down past their shoulders and let their beards sprout all over their face like Spanish Moss. Her grades, always good before, went into the cellar.

"You need to study more," I'd fret.

"Who cares about that? Grades don't mean anything. It's just society trying to put artificial measurements on us."

"There's nothing artificial about wanting to do well in life."

"Yes, there is. There's lots more important things than success."

She tried to talk to me about free love and throwing off the chains of tradition. She tried to explain how people could live magical lives where they didn't work for what they needed, the "Universe" provided it and everyone shared what they had with

176

everyone else. When she started these conversations, her voice took on a hard gloss of arrogance, and she'd talk down to me like an idiot child too duped and stupid to understand her wisdom. She ought to respect my age and experience, I thought, even if I'm not all that sophisticated.

"Who's this 'Universe'?" I asked. "How does empty space and stars give you the things you need? I know where this is coming from. I've heard about those hippies in the city. You stay away from all that. Those people are dangerous. They take drugs and who knows what-all. You're safe right here at home."

"I don't want to be safe. I want to be free."

So she set about becoming free, which mostly meant free from Virgil and Momma and me, free from our rules and restraints. She stayed out late. She came home glassy-eyed and laughing too hard. Finally, one summer, she simply left. We found out later she'd walked down to the highway and stuck out her thumb, catching rides with strangers to get to San Francisco, the big city. She lived on the street there, sleeping wherever she could find a roof, with any boy that'd take her in, and ate free stew that people gave away in the park made out of vegetables gleaned out of garbage bins.

We were frantic with worry. We called all her friends' parents, and when they all said they didn't know anything, I even called Gilly's Ma.

"I've not seen that girl. Don't talk to me about her. She's bad through and through just like her Mama."

"She's your own granddaughter."

"She's no grandchild of mine. My boy never had no child like her."

"Well, if you should hear of her, would you call us?"

"I won't hear." And she slammed down the phone.

So Virgil went down to the Sheriff's office and told the police we were missing a child.

"Kids all over the place are running away," they said. "We'll open up a police report, but don't expect a miracle."

***

The Lord was good to us. We feared Joleen might be gone forever, or even dead, but three months later, we got a collect phone call from San Francisco.

"Auntie Sairy?" she said.

"Joleen? Oh child! Do you have any idea how worried we've been? Where are you?"

"I'm in San Francisco."

"San Francisco! Good heavens, child, that's hundreds of miles from here. What on earth are you doing there?"

"I met up with some beautiful people," she said. "They gave me a ride. They said we could live here for free. They said magical things were happening here and everybody who's anybody was going to San Francisco. So it was really great at first, Auntie Sairy, but it's getting cold and the place where I was staying they kicked us out of. Can you and Uncle Virgil come and get me?"

"Of course, child. Of course we will. Virgil! It's Joleen on the phone! She's in San Francisco!"

"Okay, Auntie Sairy. I have to go now. I'm at a pay phone and someone else wants to use it."

"Don't go, child. I'm just sick for the sound of your voice. Where can we find you?"

"I have to go. I'll give you an address where you can meet me."

By the time Virgil got in, Joleen had already hung up. We wasted no time calling the neighbors to watch the stock while we drove to California to get Joleen. Virgil delayed us long enough for me to pack a hamper full of food. I didn't want to wait one minute, but he finally told me, "We don't want to have to stop on the road, do we?" That convinced me. I didn't think I could stand sitting in a restaurant thinking about Joleen starving in San Francisco. The whole way down, I sat in the car gnawing my fingernails, terrified we'd get there only to find an empty house.

"Hurry," I said. "Drive faster."

"Honey," Virgil said, "We're already going the speed limit. You have to calm down. We're getting there as fast as we can. You're going to make yourself sick."

When Virgil let me drive right through the night after he started falling asleep at the wheel, I knew he was as worried as I was. We didn't stop driving until we found the address she'd given us, a shabby old house with peeling paint on a block of houses decked out in garish colors.

The house was full of kids. Boys and girls wore their unkempt hair snarled halfway down their backs, and not a one of them seemed to have any shoes.

The boy who answered the door was thin, and his bony knees protruded from large holes in his jeans. "Joleen's not staying here, man" he said.

"Well, where is she, then? She told us to meet her right here."

"I dunno," he shrugged. "Maybe she'll be by later. Hey, Fawn! You know where Joleen is?"

"Nah. Who is it?"

"It's her parents."

"Oh, she told me they were coming." Fawn came to the door. She was almost indistinguishable from the boy we'd been talking to, as thin, long-haired and dirty, and she also wore torn jeans.

"Yeah, she was staying here for a while, but she and her old man had a fight."

"Well, can't you tell us where she is? She told us to meet her here."

"Oh, she'll probably be by later. She told me you-all were coming. You want to come in?"

"No," said Virgil. "Thank you. We'll wait out front, here. Do you know anyone you can call to tell her we're here?"

"We don't have a phone, man," the boy said.

We sat outside the house and watched the barefoot kids wandering up and down the street, going, it appeared, no place in particular. Across the street, a few sat on their porch steps, smoking a hand-rolled cigarette which they passed back and forth until they couldn't even pinch it between their finger and thumbnails any more. Deep, loud music came pouring from the front door, and the kids sitting on the porch tapped their feet in time to it, now passing around a bowl of food instead of the cigarette.

"My goodness, Virgil. Would you look at those colors," I said, marveling at the bright green and red and purple painted on the gingerbread of the houses. "Nobody'd ever paint a house that color back home."

"Hippies, I guess," he said.

"I never realized they were just children," I said. "Just children, all living higgledy-piggledy in these run-down houses. Where do you suppose their parents are?"

"Hm," Virgil said.

\*\*\*

We must've fallen asleep, tired out from the drive, because it was evening when a knocking on the window woke me up.

"Joleen!" I cried, and jumped out of the car. "Joleen! Baby! Praise God you're all right!"

180

I squeezed her so hard I thought I heard her bones cracking, and Virgil, leaping out of the car and running around to my side, hugged her just as hard.

"Is my girl hungry?"

"Yes. I knew you'd bring food, Aunty Sairy. I'm starving."

She looked starving. And dirty. "What happened to all your clothes, child? Didn't you bring anything with you?"

"Oh, I got these at the Free Store," she said. "I didn't bring a lot with me.

"What's the Free Store?"

"It's a place where you can get stuff for free."

"Isn't that nice," I said. "People giving things away for free."

"Yeah, it's cool here," she said. "But it's not *all* cool. Some people," she glared at the house, "are assholes. Anyway, I don't want to talk about it, Aunty Sairy. Where's the food?"

"You just climb in the car and dig through that hamper for whatever you want. We've got sandwiches and cold, fried chicken."

"Mmmmmm.....fried chicken. You know that's my favorite."

"There's a jar of tea back there, too. Eat all you want. My goodness, honey. You need to get some meat on your bones."

Joleen cleaned out what was left in the hamper, insisting on giving the sandwiches to the kids in the house, so we had to stop twice to eat on the way home. I was agog to hear about her experiences in the big city, but she said, "I don't really want to talk about it, Auntie Sairy." So I let her be, and she curled up in the back seat and slept most of the way home.

You'd have thought she'd've had enough of freedom. Oh, she was happy to be rescued, but set in her hippie ways nonetheless. She stayed with us only a brief time before moving down to Spokane, where she got a job in an office somewhere, calling us every now and again for money. We always found it somewhere. At least, we told each other, she had a roof over her head and a decent job. At least she had shoes on her feet.

\*\*\*

Momma passed away not too long after Joleen moved to Spokane. She'd been ailing for a while – hard life and age just caught up with her. She wasn't sorry to go, said she wasn't afraid, she was weary of trouble and ready to rest with her Savior. I spent most of my hours sitting by her bedside that last week as she ate less and talked less, and finally just curled up and stopped working like a clock whose mainspring has wound itself down.

For the last two days, we kept vigil over her without sleeping. I sang her favorite hymns and Virgil read Bible verses as she lay with her eyes half open, saying nothing, unable even to blink or grip my hand. I couldn't tell if she heard us or not, but I kept on singing just in case. Toward the end, she grunted twice, like she was trying to say something. I grabbed her limp hand and dabbed at her chapped lips with a wet rag; she hadn't even taken a sip of water for a whole day.

I don't know exactly when she slipped away. Virgil was reading the 91st Psalm, and I was watching her, when I realized her occasional, gasping breaths had stopped completely. I pushed her gently onto her back and laid my head against her chest, but heard nothing, not a stir of air, a thump of heart or gurgle of innards.

"She's gone, honey," Virgil said, and closed her eyes.

I couldn't believe it, though. I sat and held her hand, and kept on singing hymns, as the heat drained from her body. When her arm under my fingers was colder than the air in the room, I knew she'd really left us.

I laid her out myself. I sponged off her body the clammy perspiration that came over her at the end, and dressed her in her nicest things. I closed her mouth, which was gaping open because she'd had to work hard to breathe toward the end. I tied the apron I'd woven for her over her clothes, and made sure her wedding band was still on her finger.

She's buried in the cemetery on the hill and the grass is growing wild over her grave. Every spring, when the snow melts, I scatter wildflower seeds over her resting place, remembering the way she let the flowers grow higgledy-piggledy all over the farm before Virgil put most of it in timothy grass and clover. Once a month, I pull the grass away from the wooden marker Virgil made to mark the place where she lies. It's faded to silver, and the letters he gouged out with a hammer and chisel have softened around the edges:

Ida Candace Perdy
April, 1891 – September, 1970
Our Beloved Momma

Of all the people I've lost, even Cate, I felt Momma's death the most. What I did was, I absorbed her into myself. I found her words coming out of my mouth and her thoughts running around in my head. It made me happy. I didn't miss her so much when I felt I was carrying on the way she would've done.

Still, it had to change our lives. Even Virgil had come to depend on Momma's plain, good sense and practical ways. Without her, he had to anchor me all by himself. I clung to him, and he didn't fail me. Of course, he couldn't keep me company like Momma did. He had his work to do. I did the laundry alone now, and baked bread, and fixed supper by myself. There wasn't any point in keeping Momma's house up, so what we couldn't give away, the things no one needed, we moved into one room, covered against the dust, shut up the doors and windows, and locked the house. Once a year, I go over and check on the place just to make sure the roof isn't leaking.

Sometimes I sit upstairs, where Danny's bed used to stand under the window, and look toward the draw where our house stands against the backdrop of birch trees, smoke curling from the chimney. I remember crisp, winter mornings, running barefoot down the stairs, fanning the fire to a full blaze and putting on the skillet while Danny huddled under a the quilt. I remember Momma coming in from the root cellar, stomping hard on the floor to shake the snow off her boots. I remember Cate mumbling sleepily from my bed "Why are we getting up so early?" as I scooped the pile of blankets from the floor where I slept so Cate could have the bed.

It's strange how a person so solid and important as Momma could leave such a small footprint when she died. Nobody in town remembers her; it's as if she never was. But to me, she was the center of the universe, the definition of all things good. Like a sweet, sound apple, Momma was true all the way to the core. If she had her private demons, she kept them in check. She never let them run amok, as I did. She was the best thing I ever knew. Excepting maybe for Virgil.

Of course, as you already know, he's gone, too. One of the worst things about growing old is how the people you treasure drop away, leaving you standing alone like a single, rotting tree in a dead forest. The young ones carry on with their lives. They get all snarled up in the web of every-day life: passion, love, hatred, fear. Meanwhile, as age strips away one thing and then another, each of those feelings wanes. When Cate died, and Momma, and finally, Virgil, I felt the pangs of love grow dim, like seeing them through heavy smoke. Now they're gone completely. Even remembering can't rekindle them. Only one remains, the purest of all, a splinter of evil at the center of my being.

*** 

Joleen stayed in Spokane. She came up to visit Virgil and me every few months. I'd fry up a chicken and bake a batch of cookies as if she was still a little girl I could beguile with food. Virgil would come in early so we could sit in the living room together while Joleen caught us up on her doings.

"I'm taking classes at the college," she'd say. Or "I've met a new boy."

There was always a new boy. They came and went through her life like flour through a sifter.

"Tell us about this boy."

"His name is Michael, but he changed it to Starhawk."

"Starhawk? What kind of a name is Starhawk?"

"It came to him in a vision. He's a very spiritual person."

"Well, what about that Hay or Flower or whoever it was you were going out with before? What happened to him?"

"Frond. His name was Frond. I wasn't 'going out' with him, Auntie. People don't 'date' people any more. We were together. He was my Old Man. But he went down to LA two months ago to start a band. He said Spokane was too provincial and he had to explore his creativity in a more open environment."

"He just walked away and left you to start a band?"

"We weren't obligated to each other, Auntie. We're free. If I love him, which I did, I have to let him be himself."

"Gracious, Joleen. Where do you come up with these boys? Frond? Starhawk? What's wrong with ordinary names like Joe and Tom? Can't a person be himself with a regular name?"

Joleen crossed her arms and frowned. "Don't make fun of my friends. You're so...*square*, Auntie Sairy. Starhawk says a person's name should say something about who he is."

"Well, all right then, what kind of person is this Starhawk? What does he do for a living? Is he going to run down to LA to start a band also?"

"No, Starhawk is an artist-poet. He's working on a very important epic poem that will really shake up the materialist establishment."

"A poem? He quit his job to work on a poem? How long does it take to write a poem?"

"He has to wait for inspiration. Writing poetry is a spiritual discipline. You can't try to control it or you stifle the creative flow."

"Well, how's this poem coming along? When does he think he'll be done with it?"

"He's not putting any expectations on it. It has to unfold naturally, like a growing thing. It may be several volumes long, in the end."

"Joleen, who's going to read a poem that's a whole book long?"

"It'll speak to the people it's meant for."

"Well then, if he doesn't have a job, how does he pay rent?"

"He's living with me."

"Oh, Joleen, honey, not living in sin!"

"Stop fussing, Auntie. It's my contribution to art. Those who have support those who don't. The world needs people like Starhawk. He's got something important to say."

Unlike Frond and some of Joleen's other boyfriends, Starhawk became a semi-permanent fixture in her life. Not that he acted like a real boyfriend. According to Joleen, he sometimes brought other girls up to her apartment and stayed up half the night talking to them in the kitchen before they sequestered themselves in his room until three o'clock the next day.

"Don't you put up with that," I'd tell her. "Don't let him be unfaithful to you right in your own house. You give that boy his walking papers." Don't do what your Mama did, is what I didn't say.

"He explained the whole thing to me," she excused him. "He feels down sometimes. He feels like I've sold out to the Establishment. He needs input from someone who's pure."

"Stuff and nonsense. You're as pure as you need to be. He's just making excuses for his bad behavior."

"I love him, Auntie. I want him to be happy."

"What about you? Shouldn't you be happy, too?"

"I'm happy when he's happy."

Virgil and I drove down to see her when we could. It didn't happen often. She was always busy with one thing and another. After weeks of putting us off, she'd grudgingly agree to carve out some time for us as if we'd guilted her into it. Starhawk was never there when we came. I had the feeling Joleen rushed him out of the house while we were there, like maybe he was hanging around the street corner watching us enter and leave so he could avoid all contact.

Joleen's apartment was tiny, and what little furniture she'd had she'd gotten rid of after Starhawk moved in. Virgil and I sat uncomfortably on the floor, leaning against the big pillows she had lining the walls.

"Honey, you don't look so good," I told her. "Are you losing weight?"

"Maybe, a little. Don't worry about it, Auntie. I eat constantly. Star says I'm going to bloat up like a pig."

"Let me fry you some chicken."

"No, I don't want any chicken. It makes me sick to my stomach."

"Sick to your stomach? Fried chicken was always your favorite."

"It's not my favorite any more. Star and I don't eat meat. "

"Don't eat meat? What do you eat?"

"We eat brown rice and vegetables a lot."

"Well, honey, no wonder you're losing weight. I could run out and get some chicken in no time. It won't hurt you to eat it just this once."

"No, Auntie, really, I don't want it. Star would smell it in the house and he wouldn't like it. He says eating animal flesh pollutes a person's aura. It's like eating another person, he says. Animals are our brothers and sisters. He's very sensitive to things like that."

"What on earth is an aura?"

"It's the energy field you have around you. Like light, only invisible."

"Well, if it's invisible, how do you know it's there? How can you tell if it's polluted if you can't see it?"

"Oh Auntie, I knew you wouldn't understand. You have to sense it with your inner vision. Star can see people's auras. He says my aura is trashed. That's why I'm on this cleansing diet. Star can't live around people with dirty energy.

"Why, you're not dirty, Joleen. That's just ridiculous."

I looked around the house. It was clean as clean, almost sterile.

"I don't mean dirty like that, Auntie. Star is clairvoyant. He can see things in people's energy fields. He knew right away when I got...." she stopped abruptly. "Let's talk about something else, okay?"

"When you got what?" I said. Suddenly, I knew why she was looking thin, pale, and yet a little bit swollen at the same time. I knew why her walk was subtly different, and the shape of her body. I remembered these changes from the early days of Cate's pregnancy. I felt a rush of happiness. True, she wasn't married, but surely this Starhawk would do the right thing, marry her and get a job. He might be young and a little different, but he was going to be a father now. "Are you with child, Joleen?"

"'With child?' Oh, Auntie...you're so old-fashioned."

"Well, are you?"

"At the moment, yes."

"Oh, honey, that's wonderful! I'm going to be a Grandma!" Since Joleen was pacing the floor on the other side of the room and I couldn't reach her from my seat on the floor, I reached over and hugged Virgil, instead.

"No," she said flatly.

"What do you mean, 'No', child?"

"I'm getting rid of it."

"Joleen, honey. You CAN'T. You MUSTN'T. Don't do this."

"I wasn't even going to tell you. But since you already know...anyway, I'm not keeping it."

"Honey, give the baby to me and Virgil. We'll raise it." I hadn't had time even to think. I glanced over at Virgil to see what he thought, and he was nodding.

"No," Joleen said. "Star doesn't want it. He says he can't be tied down with a child. He says he's unique in the world and that's the way he wants to keep it. The thought of having a little Starhawk running around somewhere creeps him out. What if the baby grew up and came looking for him some day? It would be like meeting your doppelganger. He can't deal with it."

"Honey, I don't know what that doppel thing is. But it sounds like he just has cold feet. Once the baby is born, he'll change his mind."

"The baby isn't going to be born."

Virgil's face was getting red, and I knew he was angry. But he just got up and walked out the front door, clicking it shut behind him so quietly we hardly knew he was gone. I knew my Virgil. This was a woman's job.

"Joleen," I told her, "it's murder. You can't murder a baby just because someone else tells you they don't want it. Let us have it, honey. We'll raise it and this Star person doesn't ever have to even see it. It'll be our own. We won't even say you're the mother."

"Auntie, he's not 'this Star person'. He's my Old Man, and you and Uncle Virgil just have to accept that. Second, it's our decision what to do about this – situation, not yours. I don't believe in that whole murder thing. A woman's body belongs to herself. She's a person, not a baby-making machine."

"Joleen, honey, please don't do this. Honey, at least think about it for a while. Come back home. Let us take care of you. Give yourself some time to get used to it, to think it through. Give your young man a chance. I know he doesn't mean what he says. He couldn't want to kill his own child. Don't you two do something you'll be sorry for later."

Here's what I could've told her, but I didn't: if your Mama could've done this, could've had an abortion just as easy as you please, you'd have never been born.

"Stop talking about it," Joleen said. "Stop hounding me. I know what you're trying to do and it won't work. I love Star. I have to do what's best for the two of us."

I pleaded with her until she told me to leave.

"I can't stand it any more, Auntie Sairy," she said. "I can't stand to hear you go on and on about it. Star doesn't want it. He'll leave me if I don't get rid of it."

"But honey. You could move back with us until you have the baby."

"Just go, Auntie. Please just go." She jumped up from the floor and went into the bedroom, slamming the door behind her.

Virgil was waiting for me in the car, and I cried on his shoulder for a while.

"Sairy," he said, "you can't make up her mind for her."

"But she's wrong. She's killing her baby just because this Star person doesn't want it. She's trying to stay with him, same as Cate tried to stay with Gilly, no matter what."

"I know," he said.

After that day, we didn't see her again for months, long after she'd done the deed. And I couldn't rid my mind of the picture of that precious little baby wriggling in a cocoon of blankets in my arms, calling me "Ma". Let's face it, I told myself. She's not the only person in this world who's murdered someone.

In my mind, though the Bible says otherwise, one sin was less wicked than another. Promiscuity was bad; having a baby out of wedlock was bad, but at least it wasn't murder. Too easy to forget how one sin leads to another, anger to hatred and then on to murder, and the ones that seem small are only the iceberg's tip of the real sin, the great mother sin, that lurks under the water like a massive, dead mountain waiting to smash our good intentions to matchsticks on its treacherous shoals. Only one way we can ever be pure, and it's not eating brown rice and vegetables.

***

Joleen and Starhawk stayed together for several years. He eventually changed his name again, not back to Michael, but to Apollo. A less likely name for anyone you couldn't imagine; he wasn't much like a hero. After they'd lived together two years, I guess Joleen got sick of making excuses why he wasn't there, or maybe he made up his mind it was silly to duck around behind corners whenever we came. Joleen announced it as though she was giving us the keys to the Kingdom: "Star says he'll be home on Saturday when you come."

"Oh, that's nice, honey. Can we fix you-all some supper?"

"No, I'm going to make supper. Star's very picky about what he eats."

Starhawk (he hadn't turned into Apollo yet) met us at the door, scowling inhospitably.

"Hunh," he said, and then called back over his shoulder, "Joleen, your folks're here." He wandered away from the door without inviting us in, leaving it gaping open as if to say "Come in, if you insist." When we did, we found he'd plopped himself down on one of Joleen's big pillows with his back against the wall and was staring moodily at the opposite wall. He seemed to carry a load of resentment on his skinny frame that filled the room with tension and made him appear larger than he was.

"So," I said. "Joleen tells us you're writing a poem."

"Hunh," he said. "I don't suppose *you* read poetry."

"I don't read much," I admitted. "The Bible, is all."

"I guess that works. If you're ignorant."

"Watch yourself, young man," Virgil said. "Show some respect for your elders."

Starhawk shot him a resentful glance, but didn't look like he dared to sass him. Instead, he rose and stalked over to the kitchen door.

"Joleen! I *said* your folks are here. Get yourself out here and talk to them."

"I'm fixing supper, Star."

"Don't call it 'supper'. You sound like a hick."

"Honey, why don't you go on down to the store and get us a bottle of wine."

"Okay," he said, and without another word to us, he stuffed his hands in his pockets and left the apartment.

"He's just shy," Joleen said, coming into the living room to kiss Virgil and me hello.

"Honey, you know your Uncle Virgil and I don't drink alcohol."

"I know. But Star likes it."

"I hope he's not a drinker like – like your Mama's parents." I'd been about to say "like your Daddy," but I didn't like to mention Gilly in front of Joleen.

"Oh, he's not. But it might relax him a little," she said, returning to the kitchen.

"Where're we going to eat?" I said, looking around for a table.

"We'll just sit in the living room," Joleen said.

Supper, or dinner, as Starhawk preferred to call it, turned out to be some kind of casserole filled with rice and vegetables. It wasn't what we were used to, but we ate it to be polite, and said we thought it was mighty good.

"It's okay," Starhawk said. "But these vegetables aren't organic, are they?"

"I couldn't get all organic," Joleen said. "The broccoli isn't organic."

"I could tell," he said, and from then on, he just picked at the casserole without eating much.

"It's no wonder he's so thin," I told Joleen after supper, when he'd left again to run some errands. "The boy doesn't eat enough to keep a grasshopper alive. Can't you get him to put some meat on his bones, honey?"

"Like I said, Auntie, he's a picky eater. He says you need to be careful about what you incorporate into your body."

"The Bible says it's what comes out of your mouth that makes you impure, honey, not what you put into it."

"Well, back in those days, they didn't have all these chemical poisons, pesticides and such, on their food like we do now."

"No, I guess they didn't," I said. "Um...this Starhawk seems like a very smart young man."

"Yes," Joleen said, sounding eager, "he is. He's very sensitive, too. I'm glad you like him, Auntie Sairy."

Hmph, I thought to myself. I didn't say I liked him. I couldn't trust a drinking man, and I didn't like the way he talked to Joleen. But I let it be to keep the peace.

\*\*\*

Joleen and Starhawk never got married. He kept carrying on with this woman and that one as if Joleen was nothing more than a convenience to keep a roof over his head and food on the table. She seemed to spend a lot of time "supporting" him through various personal crises and waiting for his genius to be discovered.

I talked Joleen into showing me one of his poems, once. Of course, I couldn't make heads or tails of it. It seemed like nonsensical rambling to me, though Joleen assured me it was "innovative".

"What's he talking about?" I complained. "What's this about scavengers pecking at entrails and dark philosophies of pain? Is this boy writing about vultures? Why doesn't he write about something pretty?"

"It's a metaphor, Auntie Sairy."

"Well, if he's not talking about carcasses, then what *is* he talking about?"

"He's talking about loneliness. The agony of living in a society where you're not understood or accepted. Apollo's had a very painful life. A truly artistic person has a hard time living in a materialistic world. That's what he's writing about."

"Well, I don't see what he's got to be agonized about. How can he be lonely when he has you?"

"It's not that kind of loneliness, Auntie. It's the isolation a person with a greater, more evolved spirit feels when he's forced to live in the deadness of ordinary society."

I didn't see the greatness of Apollo's spirit; it all seemed like nonsense to me and Apollo a spoiled, selfish child. He and Virgil could barely speak to one another. Virgil, a good, old-fashioned husband, had no patience with Apollo's new-fangled "complexes", as Joleen called them, and grandiose visions of Utopia which he talked about ceaselessly but never lifted a finger to bring about. We weren't sure whether to be sorry or relieved when Apollo finally deserted Joleen for good, left her for some art director in Seattle who was more attuned to his fine sensibilities. Or maybe just had more money, Virgil said.

I worried that Joleen would do as her mother had: mourn for a bad man she loved beyond reason. But Joleen surprised me. She decided, instead, to make a fresh start in a new place. She moved down to Boise and went back to school. She got involved with a group of other women who, as she said, were "abuse survivors". What they talked about, I don't know, but it seemed to give Joleen comfort.

It also sparked some uncomfortable conversations between the two of us. She started asking me questions about her parents that I didn't know how to answer, and talking about "co-dependence".

"I don't want to talk about your father," I'd say. "I don't see any point in raking up bad memories. He was your father. 'Honor thy father and mother.'"

"But Auntie Sairy," she protested, "There are things I need to know. There's a lot of stuff I don't remember. Like, for instance, I remember a big fight one night where Daddy pulled my hair and hit me. But I don't remember why. What started it? Didn't Mama tell you about it?"

I was there, I thought, but I didn't tell Joleen that. How could the child not remember? But if she didn't, maybe it was for the best. "I don't know that she did," I said.

"Well, there must've been other times you know about. Didn't Mama and Daddy fight a lot?"

"They didn't always get along like me and your Uncle," I admitted. "They were two high-tempered people. But child, you spent plenty of time with us, too. Can't you remember the good times instead of trying to rake up all the bad?"

I guess I didn't realize then how the bad stands out. I didn't realize how one bad thing can overwhelm a hundred good ones. It's the bad that marked Joleen, not the good.

"Well," she said, "then tell me about Mama. What was she like? I remember her getting all dressed up to go out. I remember her pretty clothes. But what about us, her and me? Why don't I remember the things we did together? Were we close? What did we do?"

"Oh, child, that's ancient history. I guess you did what mothers and children do. Your Mama was a special person. She had her own way of doing things."

"But she wasn't happy, was she?"

"I guess she was as happy as anyone," I lied.

"Auntie Sairy, you're as close as a clam. I know there are things that went on. I need to know about them. Did Daddy – you know, molest me?"

"Joleen!"

"Well, did he?"

"Of course not, honey."

"Why do you say 'of course'? I know lots of women whose fathers molested them. It happens a lot more than you think."

"Honey, let's not talk about this. Your Daddy may not've been the best father in the world, but he did not do *that*."

"Okay, but I hope you see how important it is to be honest about these things. How can I regain my trust in men if I don't face what really happened?"

"Honey, I don't understand all this you're talking about. If a man is trustworthy, why then, you trust him. You trust your Uncle Virgil, don't you?"

"I guess so. I mean, yes. Of course I trust Uncle Virgil. But he's not my father."

"Well, instead of digging up what's over and done, you need to concentrate on finding a man like your Uncle. Then you won't need to worry about trusting him."

Oh, Auntie Sairy...there aren't too many men like Uncle Virgil around."

That's a fact. There aren't too many.

## Chapter 15

# Swallowed Up in Light

Virgil didn't pass until we'd crossed over the hill between middle age and old. He wasn't old like I'm old now, but we lived a good, full life together. He was ailing for several years before his passing, his heart, the doctor said. We couldn't get down to see Joleen but once every six months or so, but we loved the drive. We'd dawdle, spend the night in Grangeville, stop three or four times on the way to picnic by the lake or watch people rafting down the Salmon River.

Joleen finished school and got herself a good job. She married and then divorced, still childless. We went to Boise for the wedding, and every so often she'd make her way up to see us. She treated us like aging parents, and we were. Her life was full of imperatives we couldn't understand as we drifted cozily into the backwater of old age, where meals and arthritis and the inner workings of your own body become the loudest demands in your life. I've lost track of what-all she's up to now. She doesn't tell me as much as she used to. All I do know is, she never found her Virgil. She never settled down and had children. She's still looking for something that seems to elude her. The same nagging discontent I used to see in Cate, I see now in Joleen.

I guess that's the thing that bothered me the most: Joleen searching for something she didn't understand and couldn't find. I hoped my own child would never feel that way. All the wickedness I did for her sake didn't seem to change the road she had to walk.

I was sorry for Joleen, sorry she'd never found what Virgil and I had. We wouldn't have known how to live without each other. But then, we always were well matched, like a team of oxen yoked together and pulling side by side to get the plow across the field. Although Virgil'd never been much of a talker, I could always tell what he was thinking. We were raised in a simpler time, when men and women knew what was expected of them. There wasn't any modern confusion about who wears the pants in the family, but at the same time, Virgil knew he needed me as much as I him. Nowadays, I hear young women complaining about not being respected and all, and I can see why that'd bother them, how unfair it is. But this idea that the old-fashioned ways can't work, I don't see that. I respected and obeyed Virgil, and he loved me as his own body, just as the Bible says it should be.

After Virgil's passing, I let the place go back like Momma had it before. As she used to say, it was too much work for a woman alone to keep up. When the pine seedlings started taking over the fields where Virgil'd planted Timothy grass and clover, I threw out flower seeds and just let things grow as they would. I sold off the cattle, hogs and rabbits. But the chickens, I kept. We'd had chickens since before I could walk. I wouldn't know what to do with myself if I couldn't hear them carrying on in the morning as if a weasel'd gotten into the hen house, though there wasn't a thing going on more alarming than a few eggs being laid.

The house Virgil built stayed snug and strong. When I die, I'll leave it to Joleen, though I doubt she'll do anything with it. Sell, it, most likely. They'll bulldoze these houses into the ground to make room for something new and fancy, with city water and indoor plumbing, and heaps of electric gadgets in the kitchen. You'd think it'd make me sad, but I don't care. My memories are what gives the place life. Once I'm gone and nobody remembers how it was, it'll be nothing more than dirt and wood. Ashes to ashes, dust to dust.

Only one thing about leaving the place makes me sad: Cate's ashes will be forgotten, maybe even buried under a house or a driveway. Though, come to think of it, maybe she'd be happy about that. Maybe she'd like to have a nice, new house built over her remains. She always wanted to live in a big, fancy house.

Virgil asked that I till him into the back hay field, but I didn't do it. For one thing, I couldn't run that old tractor without Virgil to baby it along, and for another, I wanted to lie beside him, and there's no one left to scatter me over the field when my time comes. I talked to Joleen about it once, but she said she thought handling a dead person's ashes was "creepy", and I wouldn't want to burden my girl with such things. So I bought us a plot in the cemetery near Momma, and had Virgil buried there with a headstone that's half blank. My name can go on the other half.

With Virgil gone, I had a lot of time on my hands. It didn't seem necessary to get the fire going early, not unless it was cold, and I made do with a cup of tea instead of a full breakfast. The bread didn't go so fast, so I baked only every couple of weeks. And if I didn't get around to making supper, well, I was old and didn't need to stuff myself with meat and potatoes every day, anyhow. I let the garden get smaller every year, and I didn't can so much. Nor did I put up gallons of applesauce or pears and plums.

Instead, I spent a lot of time rocking on the porch. I lazed in the sun. I watched the clouds drift over the face of the mountains. I listened to the brook gurgle in the draw, if the season was right, or the frogs, or the birds, or the crickets. There's always plenty to see and hear up here, if you have any time to pay attention to it. This country is like a peaceful spell that soaks into your soul.

At the same time, with nothing else to occupy my mind, I began to think back across the years. When I lived them, they rushed by in a mad torrent, and all I had time to do was try to stay afloat through one thing and then another. Now, they began to unlock secrets and reveal subtle motivations. I started to think about the why and what of things.

I compared time to the surface of a river: when you look at it from above, you see things distorted by the moving water. When you dive under the water, though, what looked flat and opaque from above now reveals new perspectives: rocks towering above rocks, blue caverns of heavy water falling away to a distant bottom. That's what happened when I started examining my life. I started seeing patterns. What I thought of as isolated events were revealed as long strands of cause and effect that reached back to the beginning of memory.

In these mental wanderings, I came to see the roots of Joleen's restlessness, and it scared me. I wanted to warn her, to keep her from following her mother's destructive path. "Learn from the past," I wanted to say. "Don't make the same mistakes she did. Or I did." But how could I do that without telling her what I'd done, revealing the true story of Cate and Gilly, who, as it happened, neither wanted nor loved her. She was an accident.

No, she was not an accident. She was made on purpose to satisfy *my* restless yearning. She was born to fill the empty space in my heart.

What do I tell her? "I wanted a baby and couldn't have one, so your Mama had one instead, a baby she didn't want and couldn't love?"

"After I'd brought you into the world, against the will of your mother and father, I killed them both so I could have you for myself?"

When it came right down to it, I still couldn't give her up. I wouldn't turn her love for me, or fondness, or trust, at least, in the innocence of my heart, into fear and loathing. I wouldn't.

So instead of telling the story, I started to weave. It was a way to pass the time. I could hitch the end of my loom to one of the posts that held the porch roof up, and sit in the sun, enjoying all the sounds I love so well and keeping my hands busy at the same time. I didn't start out to make anything particularly elaborate. I just started randomly weaving.

***

The piece grew as the years grew. I wove it in sections, because weaving a piece more than a couple of feet wide on a back-strap loom is difficult, and over three feet wide is almost impossible. The weaver's body weight isn't enough to put an even tension on all those warps. So the wider pieces have to be woven in sections and stitched together afterward, and that's what I did. I wove section after section. I never hurried. When my eyes burned or my vision blurred, I stopped. I wanted to see every thread with perfect clarity. When my hands ached and my knuckles swelled, I didn't weave at all, sometimes for weeks.

I'm a dream weaver. I could no more weave a web without entwining my thoughts in it than I could wake up in the morning without opening my eyes. So I dreamt, and I remembered, and I wove, and the web took shape.

I took my time with it. What else have I got? Now, I've beaten the last weft in place and tied off the last warp. The web is utterly without flaw. It gleams in the light of my old, kerosene lantern, the one I prefer to electric lights now that convenience isn't as important as when I had real work to do. Its background is as pure white as the snowberries that dot the bushes along the edge of the woods in autumn.

I've woven into it the tale I've told you, the one I dared not tell Joleen. These soft threads are Danny and Momma and me cuddled up around the stove on dark winter mornings. These glowing ones are Cate, the ethereal, golden child, and these brassy ones are Cate the grown-up, tarnished and broken. This earthy, homespun wool is Momma, and this is Virgil, a sturdy bass note supporting all the rest. And here is Joleen, woven all through, even from the very beginning, long before she was born, my child, the love I longed for, the love I schemed for, the love for which I gladly lied, and manipulated, and gave up my innocence.

But what is this other presence woven all through it, a presence dark and toxic? It's Gilly, of course. How could he not be there? Although I never tried to exclude him, and wove the story faithfully, just as it happened, I didn't know he'd permeate the whole thing like the reek of cyanide vapor. I didn't expect he'd take what I intended to be the expiation of my sin, my recompense, my tale of wisdom and warning, that I wove for my daughter's protection, and make it deadly. I thought he was just another part of the story. Now, it turns out he was the whole thing, or half of it, at least. The two of them were there from the beginning: Joleen and Gilly, grasping and rebellion, desire and hatred, love and sin.

Obviously, I can't give it to her. All the pain I wanted to spare her would come pouring out of it in a poisonous cloud and kill whatever chance at joy she's got left. I'm a little sad about that. This is the most perfect thing I ever wove, the truest thing, and it turned out to be fatal. Which means there's only one thing to be done with it.

So I put aside the web and start chopping up kindling for one last time. It takes a while; my old fingers ache as the hatchet falls and I need three blows to split one stick. Once the kindling is split, though, it doesn't take long to build the fire. 80 years of practice make it an easy task. Within an hour, I have the iron stove glowing faintly red.

I take the web that's occupied so many hours these later years, my best and purest work, and cast it into the fire. I watch it twist, smolder and begin to blaze: all the memories, all the good intentions, all the evil deeds vaporize and become a pile of fine ash that drifts down through the grate and settles with the detritus of a hundred other fires on the floor of the stove. Now my passion is all one with the ashes of fires built for no greater purpose than to make tea and toast.

Joleen'll never see it. And she'll never know the real story of her mother and father, nor the real story of her Auntie Sairy, the naïve, the simple, staunchly rooted in old-fashioned religion. Auntie Sairy, the Godly. Auntie Sairy, the murderer. If I could tell her without ripping her heart to pieces, I would, but some things are better left unsaid. And in dream weaving, the truth will out; it can't be changed to suit the weaver's fancy, and it can't be concealed. I consigned my greatest work to the fire to give Joleen the only protection I have left to offer: my silence.

I let the stove go out, and the house grows chilly as the hours pass. I sit and rock in the glow of the lamp, doing nothing, only thinking of my work vaporizing in the now-dead blaze. I'm old. I've given the best and the worst I have to offer; there isn't anything left to do.

It's late when I rise from my chair and shuffle off to the bedroom I once shared with Virgil. I take the lamp with me, but don't need it. I could walk through this house, or put my hand on anything in it, with my eyes closed. I'm just ready to put on my nightgown when I change my mind and lie on top of the quilt, gray and threadbare, in all my clothes. I won't bother to change into my church dress. It's more fitting, I think, to wear the clothes I labored and lived in.

Of later years, I like it good and warm, like most old people, but I don't bother to pull the quilt over myself to keep off the chill. Soon, it won't matter. I've no idea who'll find me, or when...I haven't had regular visitors in many years. Someone'll come, eventually. Someone will call Joleen and tell her I'm gone.

I reach over and turn the lamp all the way down. My life, and all its passion, has now become nothing. I lie on my bed in my empty house, and let the voices of those I loved and wronged, the voices that the monologue of my telling and weaving have kept at bay for so long, wash over me...my ears are flooded with their babbling tide.

In the dark, I begin to whisper the Lord's Prayer. When I get to the part that says "Thy will be done," my voice falters and I struggle to go on. My will. Bent under the weight of the Church's teaching, but never truly surrendered. I am a good woman with an evil heart.

Gilly's face floats before me in the darkness, contorted with rage, and my rage rises up to answer it.

"Was I so bad?" he seems to ask me. "Are we so different?"

"Yes!" I cry. "I was no drunkard. I didn't beat up my child. I tried my best to do right."

"Tried?" he scoffs. "You *tried*? How do you know *I* didn't try?"

"You were a wicked man! An adulterer! A brute!"

"And you are a wicked woman." I'm weeping now because I know he's right. "Do you really think there's a scale where your good intentions are weighed against the bad, and if the good wins out, you earn your way to heaven? Get real," he mocked. "Come with me. I'll show you what your good intentions are worth."

"No," I say. "I don't want to. I believe in mercy."

"Did you give me any?"

"No."

"Do you deserve any?"

"No. I don't deserve it. But," I say to him, trying to reach his ruddy face with my hand, which won't move off the bed, suddenly desperate to touch him with a tenderness I never felt before, "I'm asking you for it anyway. Forgive me, Gilly."

The Dream Weaver

There's a light behind him, now. It floods the room with such a brightness as I've never seen, a brightness that burns my bones. The image of Gilly twists, smolders and begins to blaze, and gradually becomes a pile of fine ash, and finally, even the ash is swallowed up in light.